Alison pretended not to notice Benjamin Lamar striding toward her.

Ignoring him was a challenge, considering he was tall, tanned and very easy on the eyes.

"Excuse me! Dr. Stone!" he called out, trotting to her side.

"What do you want, Mr. Lamar?"

"I wanted to thank you for bringing my son Ethan safely home to me. You righted my world when you hoisted him out of that canyon, and I'll never forget your bravery."

At first, Alison didn't know what to say. Then her brain kicked in.

"Your son's condition is not my area of expertise, but it took me less than sixty seconds to realize how terrifed Ethan is of being left alone or sent away. Any idiot who feels sending him to a wilderness camp was a good idea should be used for a punching bag."

Ben folded his arms, stretching his black T-shirt across a broad chest. Then he raised his chin and stared down at her. His eyes were dangerous slits of blue ice.

"*I'm* the idiot who thought sending Ethan to camp was a good idea."

Books by Mae Nunn

Love Inspired

Hearts in Bloom
*Sealed with a Kiss
*Amazing Love
*Mom in the Middle
*Lone Star Courtship
A Texas Ranger's Family
Her Forever Family

*Texas Treasures

MAE NUNN

grew up in Houston and graduated from the University of Texas with a degree in communications. When she fell for a transplanted Englishman living in Atlanta, she moved to Georgia and made an effort to behave like a Southern Belle. But when she found that her husband was quite agreeable to life as a Born-Again Texan, Mae happily returned to her cowgirl roots and cowboy boots! In 2008 Mae retired from thirty years of corporate life to focus on her career as a Christian author. When asked how she felt about writing full-time for Steeple Hill Books, Mae summed up her response with one word: "Yeeeee-ha!"

Her Forever Family
Mae Nunn

Steeple
Hill®

Published by Steeple Hill Books™

STEEPLE HILL BOOKS

Steeple
Hill®

Recycling programs
for this product may
not exist in your area.

ISBN-13: 978-0-373-81470-1

HER FOREVER FAMILY

www.SteepleHill.com

Printed in U.S.A.

The King will reply, "I tell you the truth: whatever you did for one of the least of these brothers of mine, you did for me."

—*Matthew* 25:40

This story is dedicated to my big sister, Pam Hruza. From my very earliest memories she's been like a second mother. She has prayed for me, defended me, given me medical advice, taken me shopping, taken me trick-or-treating (again) the day after Halloween, and moved me more times than I can count. She's hauled a chaise lounge for me from Houston to Atlanta on top of her minivan, told me when to hide my eyes during scary movies, loaned me money, loaned me clothes, loaned me her car, and she would loan me her Harley if I was brave enough to get on it. She's cooked holiday meals for my family, cared for my baby daughter (now twenty-four) so I could sleep on the weekends, loved me without question or judgment when I didn't deserve it and never once expected anything in return. She is a faithful Christian, a gifted caregiver and a selfless friend, sister, mother and wife. Gail and I love you, Pamela Kay! The three of us share a boundless bond only sisters can understand.

Acknowledgments

Thanks to Grand Canyon Rescue volunteer Candace Hesson for her invaluable guidance during the writing of this story. If there are any technical errors in the opening scene they are mine alone.

Thanks to author Jill Nutter for her honest input on living with mental illness in the family.

Thanks to Coldwell Banker Realtor Mary Butler for answering all my questions and for providing me with photos of San Angelo.

Thanks to Steeple Hill senior editor Melissa Endlich for making me a better writer.

And, as always, thanks to my husband for loving me enough to waltz me across Texas, over and over again. Together we discover the settings and the characters that come to life in my stories. You make it all worthwhile, Michael!

Chapter One

Doctor Alison Stone dangled five hundred feet above the limestone canyons of Big Bend National Park, her harness secured to the bottom of a Bell Ranger helicopter. The roar from the engines was deafening, but with countless long line exercises to her credit Ali's concern was not for the din from the ship overhead but instead for the boy who'd been discovered in the small clearing below. As they approached she kept her eyes on the motionless figure, praying this mission would end in a patient rescue and not a victim recovery. Her heartbeat was normal; her hands steady where they clutched the basket litter to secure it in the sixty-mile-per-hour wind wash from the props. She had complete faith in her crew, certain

Harry and Sid would deposit her gently on the rocky ledge and then return when she called for pick up.

The search for fifteen-year-old Ethan Lamar had gone on for three days. *Three days.* Seventy-two hours with the diamondbacks, bobcats and coyotes was a minor survival exercise for a *normal* hiker. For a boy with Asperger's syndrome, being without supervision in the wild could be a death sentence. A tragic outcome she knew only too well.

Congressional hopeful Benjamin Lamar had managed to keep his son's diagnosis a private matter for over two years. But when the former Dallas Cowboys linebacker turned positive-thinking guru went to the media to plead for search volunteers, his personal drama became public fodder.

Ali's life's mission was to rescue young people, but this situation had her struggling with how to respond. Fortunately, prayer left her with no room for doubt or recourse. She cancelled her clients for the coming week, loaded her dog, a Rhodesian Ridgeback, into the Land Rover and the two best friends rushed from their home in San Angelo to the search site. As a woman who'd grown up alone in foster care and knew the firsthand, bottomless pain of losing her family, Ali's soul ached for the boy. As a psychotherapist who'd written her graduate thesis on the little-known disorder of Asperger's, she was drawn by the case and the cleverness of the missing kid.

She'd learned that although he was easily startled by the noise of kitchen appliances, he'd been brave enough to leave undetected from a camp for special needs boys, and throughout the weekend Ethan Lamar had eluded the party of rescue workers. But Monday's first search plane had spotted and confirmed a body wedged in the steep canyon.

Ali blessed Harry's experience as a pilot when he positioned her directly above the ledge and lowered her as planned. With her boots secure on a slab of rock she detached her harness and the litter from the cable. Two pats to the top of her helmet where her braid was tightly tucked signaled *all clear* and the ship pulled away, leaving her in the breathtaking silence of the national park.

Sixty vertical feet separated her from the young man curled on his side facing the cliff. His chin was pulled to his chest, his hands cupped over his ears.

"Lord, please don't let me lose another boy," she begged for Ethan's life while she secured webbing to a boulder to form an anchor. She lowered her equipment and then rappelled down the steep incline, dropping less than three feet from her patient.

"Ethan?" She forced herself to remain calm. No response.

"Ethan!" Ali called his name louder as she pressed her fingers to his neck. A weak pulse throbbed beneath the scraped skin.

"Thank you, Father." Gratitude thumped in her chest as she put on a thin pair of latex gloves.

She cautiously rolled the slender but solidly built teen to his back. One leg twisted unnaturally and he cried out.

Her gaze ran the length of his filthy jeans as she noted dried blood caked at his right ankle. His canvas high top was wedged in a crevice, shackling him to the spot.

"My goodness, kiddo. How long have you been stuck like this?" With a careful twist and a sharp tug she dislodged the sneaker, then one pass of her EMT knife blade revealed his bare leg. She made note of an orderly row of thin pink scars, then leaned closer to examine fresh purple contusions and a jagged gash that needed a couple of stitches.

"Possible head trauma, lacerations but no obvious breaks." She prepared to make a report. She reached for her cell and shifted her weight to stand.

"Stop!" Ethan grasped her wrist, then immediately let go as if the touch had burned his hand. His eyes had sprung wide. "Don't leave me!" he pleaded, his voice raspy.

"Hey, Ethan," she kept her words soft and her manner calm as she moved closer to soothe the boy. "My name is Ali. I'm a volunteer with West Texas Rescue and I'm here to take you home. But first I have to call base. Your dad needs to know you're okay."

"He doesn't care," Ethan insisted, shielding his face at the mention of his only parent.

"Of course he does. He's been worried sick. Lots of people have been looking for you," she explained.

"He'll try to talk me into going back to that camp."

"Is that why you've been hiding from us?"

"Sorta." Ethan hitched one shoulder.

"I won't let him send you back there," she assured the youth, hoping she could keep her promise. But thirty-seven years of life had taught Ali a bizarre lesson: parents could be unpredictable and downright cruel at times. Standing in the gap for kids when the worst happened had been her life's work since the day she was licensed to practice.

She reached for Ethan's hand, noting how he pulled it to himself to prevent the touch. "We need to get you some medical attention, so you're gonna have to take a ride in a noisy helicopter. Will that be okay with you?"

"If you'll stay with me." His pupils were tiny in the bright daylight, the blue of his eyes as intense as the sky above them. He squinted hard waiting for her answer, looking so much like his handsome celebrity father.

"Girl Scout's honor." She gave the three-finger salute, then used her cell to call base camp. "I've got the patient. He's scraped up pretty good, but he's talking. Send the ship and drop Sid for me. I'm gonna need some help with the litter." Her message was confirmed and before snapping the phone shut she added, "And tell Mr. Lamar I'd like a few minutes with him at the E.R."

"I'm thirsty," Ethan's pleading turned to complaining.

"We'll get you some water soon." There was a bottle in her backpack, but she didn't dare offer it for fear of air sickness during the lift.

"I hear you're quite the amateur geologist." Knowing it was Ethan's compulsive area of interest, she asked the question certain it would distract him. While he croaked about the instability of igneous rock she made the best overall assessment possible considering his reluctance to being touched. She checked his blood pressure and heart rate, splinted his ankle to prevent further injury and covered open cuts with butterfly bandages.

"The good Lord was watching over you, Ethan," she assured her patient, wondering how on earth he'd managed to stay free of swarming bugs and deadly cactus. "You know legend says that after God created the rest of the world, he dumped the leftovers in Big Bend. Just about everything out here either bites, jabs or stings."

"I only wanted to see the hoodoos." Ethan referred to the majestic volcanic columns whittled by thousands of years of wind and water.

In his fifteen-year-old mind the reason for leaving the safety of the compound was probably that simple—he wanted a closer look. But to Ali's way of thinking Ethan's inability to judge rationally was precisely why he had no business in a wilderness area, no matter the reputation of the staff who supervised the campers. The fool who recommended this therapy should be tarred and feathered. She had every intention of sharing her opinion with the boy's father as soon as they met face-to-face.

In the distance four blades thumped hard, bringing the ship closer with each turn of the rotor. Ethan shivered and covered his ears. Alison prayed for the means to comfort him during the flight and the words to address his father. She wouldn't have to wait long for her conversation with the Texas football legend who was known to claim anything could be overcome as long as you maintain the right attitude.

The doors of the E.R. whooshed open at the touch of Ben's foot on the sensor pad. He'd hoped never to return to this medical center again, but as the Proverb says, "A man plans his course but the Lord determines his steps."

On the night of his wife's fatal accident Ben had entered through the same doors, soaked through by the pouring rain, refusing to accept anything but positive news. But the next morning when the sky cleared and the sun came up over San Angelo, he was a widower and the single parent of a son recently diagnosed with a misunderstood form of autism.

Two years later and he was back again. After signaling for the police escort to wait outside, Ben strode past the information desk trying to ignore the looks of recognition that turned his way. His gaze scanned the hallway for familiar uniforms that would identify the air rescue personnel. The one-of-a-kind orange chopper on the medical center's helipad confirmed they were still present. As soon as Ben saw for himself that his son was okay, the next order of business was to thank the man who'd secured Ethan in that basket and then dangled with him from the end of a thin cable during their lift out of Big Bend.

"Mr. Lamar?" A female called from the triage area.

"Yes, I'm Ben Lamar," he answered the nurse.

"Your son's in number eight, sir." She held the door wide and motioned for him to enter. "Right this way."

"How bad are his injuries?"

"The doctor will answer all your questions."

Ben followed her a dozen steps down the hall. She stopped beside a treatment cubicle identified with a black number eight plaque overhead. Once more he was cast back to the night God had stolen Theresa away—the blood, the machines, the effort of the medical staff, the ultimate hopelessness.

Father, why have you brought me this moment again?

Before Ben was fully prepared for whatever sight might assault him, the nurse grasped the curtain and swept it aside. A physician in green scrubs bent from the waist applying the final stitches to close a gashed shin. When he stood to reach for a pair of scissors the patient became visible. Seeing Ethan propped in a sitting position next to a lovely redheaded EMT subdued the avalanche of fear Ben had been fighting back with a snow shovel.

His first instinct was to rush to his son's side and smother the boy with a bear hug. But for the last three years instinct hadn't been worth the spit it took to lick an envelope. At least not when it came to dealing with Ethan. It was as if the onset of puberty had drained his son of all common sense. The once popular kid's eccentric behavior couldn't be explained away. He seemed to have lost all ability to interpret facial expressions and tone of voice. No matter what the words conveyed, the translation in Ethan's mind was literal. While his peers socially matured Ethan didn't seem to.

His hearing had become even more acute. The sudden noise from a can opener or electric mixer could send him hiding in his room for hours. Ben could only imagine Ethan's terror while swinging from a cable beneath a roaring helicopter.

"Hey, buddy," Ben kept his voice low and nonchalant as he'd been taught by the most recent in a long string of therapists. "It looks like you're almost patched up and ready to go home."

"That's a fact," the E.R. doctor answered. "This young man needs a few days of rest and he's got stitches in a couple of places, but he's otherwise in good shape and quite a brave patient." The doctor moved aside to give Ben clear access. But two steps closer earned him a threatening growl from a menacing-looking brown dog that stood on long legs in the corner of the room.

"What is that mongrel doing in here?" Ben

demanded, backing away. He and dogs were incompatible, like the Cowboys and the 49ers.

The redhead seated beside Ethan's gurney rose to her feet and gave a brief command. "Simba, down."

The animal complied. The growling stopped.

"For your edification, Mr. Lamar, Simba's a full-blooded Rhodesian Ridgeback and since she's a licensed rescue animal she's clear to accompany me everywhere I go."

Color shot through her lovely cheeks, her eyes flashed amber sparks. Ben knew the look of a lioness defending her cub.

"I see. Well, thank you Miss—" he waited.

"Stone. West Texas Rescue."

"Miss Stone." He took the hand she extended, and her grip was firm. "Thanks for waiting with Ethan until I got here. Would you mind taking your dog out of the room and rounding up your partner for me? As soon as my son's released we'll be going. The sheriff was kind enough to give me a VIP escort and I don't want to keep them waiting. But I have to thank the guy who performed that incredible air rescue."

"10-4," she answered, then whispered something to Ethan that caused him to snicker.

"Simba, heel." The dog obeyed, falling into step beside her mistress with the bedraggled braid.

When the curtain jerked closed behind them the E.R. physician and Ethan both chuckled.

"What's so funny?" Ben asked. It had been a mentally exhausting few days and he was the odd man out in the joke.

"Sir, I think you're going to owe Doctor Stone an apology."

"*Doctor* Stone?"

"Doctor Alison Stone. She's not only the best child psychotherapist on staff at the medical center, she was the *guy* hanging from that chopper with Ethan today. It was Alison Stone who rescued your son."

Chapter Two

Ben hadn't chased after a woman in a lot of years. A lifetime ago the female football groupies had been plentiful. And certain women had become regulars at his speaking events. Now that a reasonable period of mourning had passed, ladies were overtly showing interest he was still not prepared to return.

But this chasing he was doing today was in the physical sense. The moment Ben realized he'd mistaken Doctor Stone for a general EMT, he'd promised Ethan he would return right away and had taken off down the corridor. A power walk turned to a trot as Ben left the air-conditioned building to be enveloped by the warm Texas afternoon. He darted for the south side of the complex in the direction of the helipad and closed the last fifty yards in an easy sprint, thankful he hadn't given up running when he'd given up the game.

Two volunteers in familiar jumpsuits stood sentry by the expensive chopper, but there wasn't a redhead with a big dog in sight.

"Excuse me," Ben called. "Do either of you know where I can find Doctor Stone?"

One of the men turned to respond, his eyes widened with the recognition Ben had come to expect but never took for granted. "Oh, Mr. Lamar, it's you. Listen, we're so grateful things worked out with your son."

"Thank you." Ben shook hands with both rescue workers. "I can't tell you fellas how much I appreciate the incredible job you did getting my boy out of danger."

"All in a day's work, sir." The man whose name tag identified him as Harry shrugged off Ben's praise. "If you're lookin' for the Rock, she and Simba are probably huntin' down a grassy spot."

"The Rock?" A play on her last name, maybe? What's the deal with private jokes today?

"Sorry," Harry apologized for the confusion that must have shown on Ben's face. "That's our nickname for Doc Stone because she's so solid under pressure, especially if a kid's involved. She wouldn't hear of anybody else making that pick up."

Ben shrunk another few inches. Not only had he insulted the lady's ability and the pedigree of her animal, he seemed to have insulted her integrity as well.

"Please, guys," he pleaded. "Don't take off with Doctor Stone on board until you know we've spoken. I might have offended her and I need to apologize."

"You got it. But whatever it is, don't sweat it too much. It takes an awful lot to rile up the Rock." Harry was reassuring.

Ben wanted to be comforted by the comment, but evidence so far was to the contrary. Something in his gut told him there was a doghouse in his future. With a natural aversion to the entire canine breed, that was the last place he wanted to be relegated. He prepared to head for the front lawn of the expansive medical plaza.

"And Mr. Lamar," Harry continued, "I want you to know you'll get my vote if you decide to throw your helmet into the ring for that Congressional seat."

"I'm counting on that," Ben answered as

he began to stretch his legs, once again back in the chase.

"Did you get my joke, Sid?" Ben heard Harry question his co-worker. "Helmet instead of hat? It's a football thing. You're a golfer. You wouldn't understand."

Ali pretended not to notice Benjamin Lamar striding toward her in fancy cowboy boots that must have cost him a pretty penny. Ignoring him was a challenge considering he was tall, tanned and very easy on the eye. The man already got more attention than the law allowed, and with good reason. He was capital H-O-T!

The last thing he needed was another drooling female.

"Excuse me! Doctor Stone!" he called out. Twenty-five yards still separated them.

The ridge of thick hair on Simba's back stiffened. She grumbled, a threatening sound deep in her chest.

"You don't care for him, do you, girl?" It was amusing but puzzling. Simba was such a lovable and easygoing hound. Her reaction signaled that she sensed the presence of danger. Or fear. Was it possible the big, bad football star could be afraid of a dog? Just in case, Ali quieted Simba with a hand signal.

"Doctor Stone." He trotted to her side, then eyeing Simba he backed up two steps. "Thanks for waiting on me."

"Actually, Mr. Lamar, I was waiting on my mongrel to do her business."

"I apologize for that comment." He lowered captivating blue eyes and ducked his head in a manner that had publicly charmed Texans for two decades. If rumor of his political aspiration was true, he'd soon be using that humble gesture to convert interested females into registered voters.

"It was a dumb thing to say, but what I know about dogs wouldn't fill a Dixie cup. There was zero chance I'd recognize a working animal."

"Hmm, and I always thought the 'Service Dog, Do Not Pet' emblem was a pretty good clue."

Probably for the first time, he took a long look at Simba and noticed her embroidered orange vest. Most people asked to pet a service animal as soon as they realized they weren't allowed to. This guy didn't. In fact, he shifted his weight away another step.

He was close to a strikeout, or whatever

football players do when they blow a big chance. Ali wasn't impressed with his sports celebrity, she thought his positive living mantra was simplistic, she didn't approve of his politics and she had reason to question his parenting skills.

"You don't like dogs, do you?" she asked.

"They don't care much for me either, so it's mutual. I don't take it personally."

"That's probably a good thing. Political campaigning requires thick skin." Something he'd need to soothe his ego when he lost if her vote counted for anything.

"Well said." He nodded. "But that's not the subject I tracked you down to discuss."

She checked her watch, knowing the crew was waiting. "If you were a paying client I'd start the meter, but the first one's always a freebie. What do you want, Mr. Lamar?"

His handsome head snapped back at the tone in her voice. Good! After what he'd put his son through, she wanted to shake the confident man till his teeth rattled!

"Since time appears to be money to you, *Doctor Stone*, I'll be brief. First, and most important, I want to thank you for bringing Ethan safely home to me." Lamar pointed toward the

E.R. "That boy is the center of my life and I've been sick with worry these past few days. You righted my world when you hoisted him out of that canyon and I'll never forget your bravery."

Now, as she bothered to look beneath the very appealing exterior, it did appear he hadn't slept in a while. Okay, it was Ali's turn to stare humbly at her steel-toed boots. Before she could ask for forgiveness for being a jerk, he hurried on.

"Second, I believe you called this meeting." He fished a scrap of paper from his pocket and unfolded it. "This says you wanted to have a word with me." He looked at his heavy, gold wristwatch. "I need to be with my son, so please make it quick."

The small amount of guilt she'd been feeling toward the famous linebacker crumbled like a vanilla wafer between Simba's molars.

"I'm a psychotherapist and I deal primarily with kids who've suffered traumatic loss or abuse—"

He held his palm outward to silence her. "Ethan already has a therapist, several in fact. If you were going to pitch your services—"

"Your son's condition is not in my area of expertise," Ali blocked his interruption with one of her own. "But it took me less than sixty seconds to realize how terrified Ethan is of being left alone or, worse, being sent away. I think it's unconscionable that your therapist suggested you allow your son to attend that wilderness camp. Any idiot who feels that was the proper way to treat Ethan should be strung up and used for a punching bag."

"Uuf!" He bent at the waist and grabbed his gut.

She had no idea how to interpret his action. "Are you in pain?" she asked the obvious.

"Only if you consider a low blow painful."

Lamar stood tall. He folded arms any man would envy, stretching his black T-shirt tight across a broad chest. Then he raised his chin and stared her down from a height that forced her to look up. His eyes were dangerous slits of blue ice.

"I guess I deserved it since I'm the *unconscionable idiot* who thought sending Ethan to camp was a good idea."

Ali's belly quaked in a way that never happened when she was suspended a couple thousand feet above the earth from the bottom of a rescue line. This person looming over her was both manly and menacing, celebrated in a sport where intimidation was a minimum daily requirement. It was his right to call the shots on treatment. Ethan was his son.

She should back down, apologize for over-stepping her bounds. Still, Ali completely dis-agreed with the man's approach and wouldn't sleep a wink tonight if she thought the boy could be sent back into a dangerous situation.

"Sir, I respect you as Ethan's father and support your right to make decisions about his future. That said, since I was engaged in his rescue I have every intention of following up on the welfare of my patient. I'll be keeping my ear to the ground for any news on this case."

"Take a number." Lamar walked away from any further discussion.

"Simba, heel," Ali called. She hurried to catch the aggravating man. "Wait up, Lamar!"

"Going my way, Stone?" He didn't as much as glance over his shoulder.

"As a matter of fact, I am. I told Ethan I'd be right back."

"I don't know what he found so funny about that."

She smiled to think she'd coaxed an appro-priate response from Ethan. "He was amused?"

"Laughed out loud. And with his weird

sense of humor that's something he doesn't do often. What did you whisper to him, anyway?"

"I told him Simba and I needed to go for a walk before one of us marked our territory right across the toes of your handmade boots."

Chapter Three

Ten days had passed and Ethan was stubbornly nursing a grudge.

"Son, you've got to leave that room sooner or later. Please come down and join me for dinner," Ben called from the top of the stairwell. Since Ethan could detect a pin dropping, there was little doubt he'd heard his father's request.

That Big Bend business with the camp and the helicopter rescue was over and done with, behind them forever. The publicity had died down, most of Ethan's scrapes were healed and the swelling in his ankle was gone. But the boy hadn't been outside the threshold of his bedroom since the E.R. experience.

Ben knew there was no bribe he could offer or threat he could make that would get his son to budge. Short of starving Ethan into cooperation there was little to do but give it time, the one thing Ben had in short supply.

As much as it irked him to admit it, that know-it-all doctor had been right when she'd called him an unconscionable idiot! Coaxing Ethan into the camping experience seemed to have set them back months of progress. Ben was not only running out of time, he was running out of places to turn for help.

His visits to online forums revealed patient coping methods he never dreamed anybody would attempt. Reading the posts by self-proclaimed *"Aspies"* was heartbreaking. There was nothing he wouldn't do to save his son from sinking further into the depths of the bizarre disorder.

"Ethan? We may have company later." Ben was winging it, determined to get a reaction.

There was no reply, nor could he detect volume from the television. Self-injury was a concern since Ethan had done his share of experimental cutting. So, complete quiet in the rooms upstairs was never a good sign.

"Ethan!" Ben called loudly, as he traveled the hallway toward the rooms where privacy was no longer his son's right. The last shred of patience snapped as Ben's shoulders filled the open doorway. "Answer me this instant!"

Ethan jumped at the sudden intrusion, brushed away his earphones and flung himself against the headboard of the bed where he'd been sitting.

"What is it?" he demanded. "Why are you always scaring me like that?"

The boy's abrupt tone and disrespectful comments were almost intolerable for Ben. He'd been reared with strict rules of etiquette and sportsmanship, had embraced them all his life. In his head he knew Ethan's rudeness was a symptom of anxiety—the boy probably wasn't even aware of the effect of his tone and choice of vocabulary—but the words penetrated Ben's sense of decency like darts pierced a bull's-eye. Every medical professional he'd spoken with had warned him to choose his battles. On the worry scale, disrespect was fairly low compared to what seemed like a budding case of agoraphobia. Ethan's refusal to leave his rooms had to be brought under control, but Ben was at his wit's end.

How could he consider moving into the political arena when his son was digging his heels in deeper every day, refusing any help? Being the single parent of a boy whose future had gone from promising to unpredictable had meant putting all personal dreams on hold. Possibly forever. How did a motivational speaker put a positive spin on that?

"I asked you a question," Ethan snapped.

"I beg your pardon." Ben attempted to contain his aggravation. A sarcastic tone would only confuse Ethan's warped decoding process. "I've been trying to get your attention."

"Well, now you have it." Ethan tightly folded his arms across his chest, unaware of his own body language, much less anyone else's. The lack of ability to send or interpret a nonverbal cue had been one of the earliest signs of trouble.

"Mrs. Alvarez made your favorite before she left for Mexico. Chicken pot pie," Ben tempted. "How about coming down to eat while it's hot? I thought we might invite company over later, maybe watch that History Channel documentary again."

Ethan leaned toward his night table, opened the top drawer and pulled out a cellophane package of peanut butter crackers. He raised the snack for his father to see, then tossed it back into the drawer where he obviously hoarded treats. "No, thanks," he muttered.

"Okay, that covers dinner. How about visitors?"

Ethan sighed, unfolding long legs that would have made him a great athlete once upon a time. He stood and turned his back, giving Ben a look at dirty hair flattened to his head. After a few steps toward his bathroom, Ethan glanced over his shoulder.

"Listen, Dad. You don't have to keep making all this effort, pretending you're not mad at me for what happened."

"You mean with the camp?" They'd covered this territory a number of times. Ben hoped the topic was closed, but nothing was ever completely finished with Ethan.

The boy's chin dropped to his chest. After several long moments he looked up, his face flushed with unspoken pain.

"I mean with Mom."

Ben shut his eyes against the comment. He shook his head, exhausted from the ever-present subject. "Please, don't go there again. Not with me anyway."

"Then with who?" Ethan demanded.

"You name it! There are any number of excellent therapists willing to come see you if you won't go to them. I've had calls from

Doctor Ackerson, Doctor Cooke and Doctor Hunter. They're all anxious to hear from you."

"What about Doctor Stone?" Ethan squinted, watching for a reaction.

Ben couldn't help admiring his son's sense of timing.

"You're kidding, of course," Ben answered.

Ethan shook his head. "I liked her," he said simply, then moved toward his dressing room, through another threshold without a door. Physically beyond his father's sight and emotionally beyond his comprehension.

Ali parked in the circular driveway of the three-story mansion that showcased Texas limestone and Mexican stucco. The foundation for the home had been blasted from a hillside and then positioned to appear as if it sprung up naturally out of the rock. In no hurry to go inside, she moved to the edge of the front terrace designed with an overhang facing west where a brilliant sunset was in progress.

"Check it out, Simba."

Alert eyes followed the direction her mistress pointed, as if understanding perfectly.

Ali had always been fascinated by the setting of the sun, a dazzling kaleidoscope unique for each day. Nothing was more breath-taking than a long line flight during the last twenty minutes of daylight. And she'd prefer the dangers of an air drop mission any day over the one Benjamin Lamar had implored her to consider.

"If this is the view Ethan has from his bedroom, it's no wonder he won't come out." She turned away from the stunning vista and moved to stand before the home's front entry with Simba close by. The dog was truly a gift from God, a family member who could never be taken away and perfect in her inability to judge the failures of her mistress.

Three sharp raps of a brass knocker brought footsteps and a large blurry figure to the inside of the frosted glass. One of the double doors swung wide and then immediately closed to a four-inch opening.

"Was it really necessary for you to bring that animal?" Benjamin Lamar spoke though the gap.

"It's wonderful to see you again, too. Thank you so much for agreeing to meet with me on such short notice." Ali hoped a snappy response would mask her self-doubt from the man so full of self-assurance.

"I asked a simple question." And evidently had no intention of inviting her inside until she responded.

"The answer is yes. Simba goes everywhere with me because she's part of the team. And since rescues can't be scheduled like football games, we're always together and prepared, even during office hours at the clinic."

"Can you put her back in your car or tie her up outside?"

Simba growled. A hand signal silenced her, then Ali offered what she knew would be a condescending smile and shook her head.

"Listen, Mr. Lamar, you all but begged me to give this a shot, so you're going to have to be flexible on this one point. Simba won't make a move without my command, she doesn't shed and she hasn't had an accident on the floor since she was six weeks old. If you're going to trust me with your son, then you ought to trust me with my own dog."

A look of resignation crossed his tanned face. He stepped back and opened the door, his hand sweeping toward the foyer, an invitation to enter. Ali inhaled slowly and moved across the welcome mat. She was greeted by a room with soaring ceilings, hand-dyed rugs over a mesquite parquet floor and cozy French country furnishings. She recalled reading his late wife had been into interior design.

"You have a beautiful place." She admired the wall of windows opposite the entry hall. "What a sensational view."

"Thank you," he answered humbly. "It's way too big for just two of us, but it's the only home Ethan's ever known. Getting him to change his socks is a chore most days, so changing our residence is out of the question for now."

Alison nodded, understanding. An Asperger kid was a creature of rigidity and order. Keeping life calm meant holding change to a minimum. His mother's death must have sent Ethan into a nosedive. He seemed to feel somehow responsible, so it was no wonder he wouldn't drop the subject that had rocked his world. Having lost her own mother to family violence when Ali was only nine years old, Ethan's irrational sense of accountability was a belief she could relate to on so many levels.

"I'm sorry I was rude at the door," Lamar apologized, keeping one eye on Simba's whereabouts. "I really do appreciate you driving out here this evening. Have you had your dinner yet? Our housekeeper makes a tasty chicken pie from scratch, but Ethan turned his nose up to it. What a shocker."

Ali heard the frustration in his words. A father wanted answers, but very often there were none. Just as there were few alternatives when living with the chaos of mental illness. And the patient always seemed to hold the trump card, the threat of self-destruction.

"Thanks for the offer, but I had a power shake on the way over." She curled her arm in a body builder's pose, pointed to her biceps and enjoyed his nod of approval. "So, where do I find that son of yours?"

"His suite is upstairs."

"Suite?" She felt her eyebrows rise.

"It's a big house, remember?" Lamar explained. "The area was originally intended for out-of-town guests. When Ethan was old enough to need more space, we thought it was a good idea for him to have a game room where his buddies could hang out. Unfortunately, my son's friends can't tolerate his OCD, and instead of games his shelves are lined with specimen samples."

"Specimens?" Her lips twisted like she'd just sucked a slice of lemon. Even in med school dead things floating in formaldehyde had creeped her out.

"You'll see" was Lamar's ominous explanation, but the sparkle in his blue, blue eyes indicated humor.

He pointed toward the steps that wound upward two flights. "Ethan's expecting you. He's on the second floor."

"How will I recognize his *suite?*"

"Just look for the rooms with no doors on the hinges. I'll be in the kitchen if you need me."

"This may take a while," Ali warned as she shifted the weight of her oversize bag and started up the steps.

"It usually does when the meter's running, *Doctor Stone.*"

She rolled her eyes as she trudged up the stairs with Simba close behind. Of course, Benjamin Lamar would make sure he had the last word.

Just like a politician.

Chapter Four

Ben watched as the lady and her dog climbed the carpeted steps. The only other time he'd seen Alison Stone she'd been in a rescue worker's one-piece jumpsuit. The zippered pockets from chest to ankle had been stuffed lumpy with recovery gear that hid her womanly curves. With her lustrous hair caught up beneath a safety helmet, it was no wonder he'd mistaken her for one of the guys.

But today in jangly silver jewelry, a bright turquoise sleeveless blouse and perfectly fitted jeans there was no doubt about her gender. She was one hundred percent female and very easy on the eye.

He cleared his throat to whisk away the direction his mind was wandering. The slight sound drew the attention of the dog. It stopped at the landing to turn a dark, searching gaze downward. Ben pointed toward Simba's attractive mistress, narrowed his eyes and mouthed the word "Shoo!" The animal complied but Ben felt certain she'd made the decision on her own and it had nothing to do with his command.

"Father, am I ever going to have a say in the direction of my life again?" He prayed aloud as he'd done a million times since the day he'd returned from Theresa's memorial and come back to the house to face Ethan's problems. Alone.

With time, the aloneness had turned to solitude and eventually the home so filled with his late wife's touch had become comforting. Where Ben found refuge in their tasteful surroundings, Ethan continually used reminders of his mother as reason to resurrect the past. Certain he bore guilt for distracting her during a rainy drive, Ethan felt he deserved the blame for her death. The assumption was as wrong as wrong could be, but it had become part of Ethan's obsessive thinking, a behavior that had Ben clutching the tail end of his frayed rope.

"Father, for forty-two years You've blessed

me with the ability to face any challenge." Ben continued his one-sided conversation as he headed across the foyer and into the fragrant kitchen. *"By now I thought we'd be operating on a Texas-size scale. But instead of wrestling legislative issues I'm struggling to get my kid to sit at the dinner table with me. What's up with that? And if the folks who used to pay their hard-earned money to hear me speak could see me now, they wouldn't be lining up to vote, they'd be lining up for refunds."*

Ben shook his head at his inadequacy, slipped quilted mitts on his hands and scooped a cookie sheet from the hot oven. He flipped one of the single-serving pies upside-down on a stoneware plate, removed the baking tin and pierced the flaky bottom crust with a fork. Steam drifted upward, lasting only a few seconds before dissipating into air stirred by the fan blades slowly rotating overhead.

You are a mist that appears for a little while and then vanishes. Ben recalled the words from the book of James.

"Okay, Lord, I get it," he admitted. *"This is temporary and there's a bigger picture that I can't see. But gaining a first down would be helpful now and again."*

Too impatient to take his plate to the table, Ben shoveled a mouthful of chicken and vegetables through parted lips. He was immediately reminded with scalding consequences that a cool-down moment and a proper grace are helpful now and again, too.

Ali walked through Ethan's rooms, amazed at the affluence that was basically lost on the boy who really only cared, that is to say obsessed, about one thing.

Rocks.

After a brief reunion they'd struck a deal, or at least she thought so. Ethan would brush his teeth and comb his hair within ten minutes and in exchange Ali would allow him to show off some of his specimens, which turned out to be an impressive collection of core samples. Putting a time constraint on Ethan's activities would give her a starting point toward measuring his OCD rituals and then she'd begin to strategize on how to hold them to a dull roar. She glanced at the large-faced, loudly ticking alarm clock she'd brought with her and noted his first deadline was approaching.

"Ethan, time's about up," she called without turning in the direction of his dressing area.

Maybe if he was cooperative she'd suggest his father reconsider the sanctity of the bathroom and agree to re-hang the door.

"The water hasn't been running long enough," Ethan answered, referring to one of his requirements that had to be fulfilled before he could begin to brush his teeth.

"You can let it run all night for all I care, but if you're not finished and back in here minus the stinky breath in three more minutes, Simba and I are going downstairs to visit with your dad and we're not coming back up tonight."

He poked his face around the door frame and held up five fingers. "I need a little longer."

"Nope." Ali shook her head. She had to take a hard line right out of the gate or she wouldn't have any wiggle room when it came time to ease up. "Ethan, it's been a long workday for me and right now Simba needs a walk more than you need to purge the plumbing. When time's up we'll be downstairs for a few more minutes. Otherwise, we'll give this a try again tomorrow. If you don't want the same results, I suggest you take care of personal hygiene before we arrive."

"There's no need to be difficult," he complained. "I don't remember you being this way before."

As she had during their first encounter, Alison noted Ethan's speech seemed normal, even above average for teens. She'd learned early in her research that language is one of the most diverse areas of autism, ranging from non-verbal to highly skilled. And while Ethan communicated well, he processed information and reacted with the behaviors of a boy half his age.

"I'm not the one being difficult, kiddo. Like I told your dad, if I'm going to spend my time driving out here, then I expect some flexibility from the two of you in return."

"If I'd known you were so bossy, I wouldn't have asked to see you."

"Is that a fact?" When her young patients wanted to spar, Ali was happy to oblige them, keeping it on their level. "Well, welcome to reality where most of the world learns to adjust. I'm here to work with you, not cater to you."

"You sound just like *him*." Ethan jerked his head in the direction of the hallway. "You're not going to start quoting his *positivisms* at me, are you?"

A swarm of barbed responses tumbled inside her brain, but she held them in check. While she hoped Benjamin Lamar would share her position on the treatment of his son, any further like-mindedness would probably be a fluke. Ali couldn't imagine finding much more in common with a man so well known for his conservative affiliations and views. Ethan's comparison was definitely not complimentary.

He stared, waiting for her response.

"Your insult is duly noted," she quipped. "And if I think of something you need to hear, I'll quote Mickey Mouse if it appeals to me."

The final few seconds ticked away and the old-fashioned bell began to clang on the top of the red enameled clock.

"So, will you wait a little longer on me?"

Knowing Ethan would likely interpret the expression incorrectly, Ali controlled the urge to pfffft at the comment.

"No, sir." She gestured for Simba to follow and both headed for the door. "Tomorrow is another day," Ali called over her shoulder. "And if you're interested, the source of that quote is Scarlett O'Hara."

Ben tipped the bottom of his glass toward the ceiling and waited for the last, stubborn chunk of ice to drop into his waiting mouth. His pallet was roasted from the molten chicken pie, but two frosty glasses of tea had eased the burn. The echo of footsteps against the wood floor caused him to turn his face toward the hallway that connected the grand entry to the spacious kitchen.

"Mr. Lamar?" The doctor called out and stepped into his field of vision.

Clunk! A frozen, pointy projectile thumped Ben's right eye followed by a cold dribble and then the smack of a mushy wet blob.

He squinted hard against the blow of the ice and then the sting of the fat lemon wedge. Though his eyes were tightly closed, his ears clearly detected snickering.

He groped for the napkin he'd tossed beside his empty plate.

"I'm sorry if I startled you." More snickering. "Do you need help, a bib maybe?"

He pressed one corner of the linen square to his eyeball and used another corner to soak up the moisture trickling down the side of his face. Ugh. Cold.

"Thank you for your generous offer," his voice was muffled by the thin layer of fabric. "I think I can manage this."

Toenails tap-danced on the kitchen tile nearby. *That dog!*

Ben dropped the napkin, swiveled his head

to the left and unconsciously pulled his knees upward in one smooth motion.

Thankfully, the animal had come to an obedient halt, not appearing aggressive at all. Still, its mere presence in Ben's personal space made his flesh shrivel. Alison Stone's smile said she was really enjoying his discomfort, as well she should. He knew his reaction was just one step below a woman jumping on a chair while she screamed bloody murder over a cockroach in her kitchen.

"You're a psychotherapist. Surely I'm not the first person you've run across with cyno-phobia." Ben's tongue began to feel fat and dry in his mouth and his pulse thumped in his ears thanks to the nearness of the animal.

"Actually, the fear of dogs is not uncommon in kids. But by your age most guys have worked through it."

"Well, until now I've been able to stay away from it so I've never felt the need to 'work through it' as you say."

With sympathy for his anxiety, she reached for the dog's collar and slid her index finger into one end of the choker chain.

"Why don't you count to ten and then follow

us outside? I'll put Simba in the Rover with the windows down for a few minutes while we talk."

Without waiting for his response the pair quietly left the room and moments later the front door closed behind them. Ben did as instructed—waited for a ten count, threw in an extra five for good measure and then moved into the front hall. His natural inclination was to throw the deadbolt and lock the infernal woman and her evil-looking hound outside. But then Ben would be no better off than Ethan, who was holed up in his bedroom, paralyzed by his fears.

Lord, Lord, Lord. Ben wondered, as he often did, if he'd passed a defective gene to his son. Theresa had been a fearless dynamo, and she'd never expressed any feelings of personal responsibility for Ethan's mental illness. Maybe that's why she'd had so much more patience with his problems.

Ben exhaled, hoping to blow away the worry, twisted the knob and pulled the door halfway open. Good to her word, Doctor Stone had secured her lion-hunting dog in the vehicle. Yes, Ben had looked Rhodesian Ridgeback up on Wikipedia. Forewarned was always forearmed, whether the opponent was a six-foot-three guard or another candidate running against you. Or, worse, a dog running at you. The little ones could turn from yap boxes to ankle-biting machines with no provocation. Ben didn't even want to consider what that hundred pounds of sleek muscle called Simba could do to an unsuspecting target.

"Maybe while we work on Ethan's problems we can address this little issue of yours as well." The doctor moved toward him, her jingling silver jewelry as complimentary and distracting as the womanly sway of her body.

"If you'd just come here alone, that'd be one less phobia on the to-do list."

She shook her head, earrings dancing. "I'm afraid that's not possible, especially at this time of year. Unfortunately, Ethan won't be the last person to need a rescue crew. Simba's not just my partner—she's part of the team."

Ben learned early in life about spittin' in the wind. Ethan needed this lady and if the truth be told, Ben did, too. If he wanted to get on with his life and into the Congressional race before it was too late, then he and his son both required a miracle worker.

He prayed the beauty before him had more than a buff arm up her sleeve.

Chapter Five

From what Ben could tell things hadn't gone well upstairs today. His wood-paneled study was on the main floor, directly below Ethan's rooms. On this third daily encounter with a new therapist there seemed to be a lot of cajoling, threatening, alarm clock jangling and disagreement between the muffled voices overhead. It was impossible to discern whether the subject matter was anything of importance or if it was just the two establishing ground rules.

Ben was a big believer in rules. They defined a fair game for the players, kept a race equal between opponents and prevented society from running amuck. Through the gift of the Bible, mankind had been given the ultimate rule book and Ben reasoned that if people would simply keep a positive attitude and follow God's guidelines, their lives would be so much easier.

It was a perfect plan in theory that humans messed up in practice.

Ben folded the national politics section of the paper he'd been reading and considered his own situation. He tried faithfully to let The Word be *the light unto his path*. Even so, his road had been far from easy with its share of hidden trip wires. Landmines exploded when he seemed least prepared to deal with a crisis.

But he'd always survived.

"I hear Ya, Lord." Ben tossed the newspaper into the recycle bin beside his favorite leather recliner. *"You never said it would be easy, but You told us we wouldn't be alone. I'm counting on You to keep that promise."*

Ben wasn't prone to self-pity because overall his life had been amazing. But the past few years had tested his mettle well beyond anything the world of professional sports had thrown his way through injuries, contract negotiations and unexpected trades. Personal tragedy had shown him how quickly life and priorities can shift, turning from a skyrocket ride toward success to a struggle for emotional survival. Entering politics would not only be the fulfillment of personal dreams and family expectations, it also would be a welcome relief to focus on the needs of others for a change.

Yesterday's call from his old college roommate had brought undeniable attention to the fact that a fuse was burning, and with or without Ben's cooperation, matters would soon be decided.

"Buddy, the deadline to put your name on the ballot is three weeks away," Randy had reminded Ben. "You will never get an opportunity like this again. With Matthews stepping down at the end of his term, it's a perfect segue for the party from one strong conservative to another. Not to mention, having your last name on the ticket will guarantee a record voter turnout."

The Lamar family had been active in Texas politics since Mirabeau Lamar served as President of the Republic in 1838. With Ben retired from football, his uncles were adamant—carrying on the tradition wasn't just an option, it was a calling. While family money and support was a given, over the years Ben had forged his own personal relationships that he'd learned could be counted on through good times and bad.

Randy Mason topped the list as more than a best friend who shared Ben's values. Randy was willing to put his successful law practice on hold to coordinate the campaign ahead.

They'd been planning this move and testing the political waters for months, but Ben had blown it.

"Man, you know we'd already be drafting phone bank volunteers if I hadn't messed things up with Ethan by sending him to that camp. Still, I'm optimistic."

"How so?" Randy asked.

"He just started working with a new therapist and I think they're getting somewhere. We might have him outside the house again soon." Ben wanted to believe his statement was positive thinking and not an outright fabrication.

"Look, Ben, you know I love your kid. But the truth is Ethan's in his own world these days. Forgive my bluntness, but as long as his physical needs are met and he's free to study his rocks, he doesn't really care whether you're on the campaign trail or downstairs in your office. You haven't had much of a life since Theresa died and it's time you thought of yourself."

Hearing his friend say the words Ben hadn't dared to speak out loud was an emotional body check. To Randy's point, strangers would surely appreciate their efforts more than his son appeared to most of the time.

Well, what about me, Father? Do my dreams count for anything, especially when I want to be of service to others?

"You still there? I hope you're not being quiet because you're mad at me for speaking my mind."

Ben had to chuckle. "No, my friend, I'm not mad. I was just enjoying a moment of agreement and then doing a little silent whining to God."

"Whining? Ben Lamar, whining?" Randy snorted laughter. "I've known you a lotta years and I've never heard you to so much as grumble under your breath, not even after the late hit that broke your collarbone in the '93 Super Bowl."

"Don't remind me." Ben pressed his palm to the old injury. "That busted bone can predict a thunderstorm more accurately than The Weather Channel."

"Don't miss my point." Randy wouldn't give up. "You've never been one to complain, so if you feel the need to let loose, just go ahead. You've earned it."

"I'll remind you of this conversation when

we get to Washington and I have a complaint *du jour*."

"Does that mean you'll commit?" The hope in Randy's voice made Ben regret the quip.

"That means I'm still praying for a positive sign that Ethan can handle change. Let's give this new doctor some time and then I'll feel better about making decisions for our future."

"Just promise me you'll keep an eye on the—"

"Calendar." Ben finished Randy's sentence. "Yes, I'm well aware the game clock is running."

A loud *whump* resounded overhead. Ben abandoned his rehash of yesterday's conversation and jumped to both feet. By the time he reached the bottom of the staircase, frantic barking echoed from the rooms above. He dashed upward while a dozen scenarios flooded his mind, all of them disturbing.

"Give up!" Ethan shouted.

"No! *You* give up!" Doctor Stone demanded over the ruckus of her blasted dog.

Nothing Ben imagined even came close to the sight that assaulted him as he stood in the doorway. Ethan's bed had been stripped of the covers. The mattress was bare, the blankets were heaped in a pile and the pillows had been flung across the room. He lay facedown on the floor clutching one corner of the sheet, holding on with all his might.

The opposite corner was in the unyielding grip of Doctor Stone, aka the Rock. Her worn, leather boots were planted wide, both heels dug into the carpet. Her cheeks were flushed from physical exertion. Strands of red-orange hair the color of a Texas wildfire had wrestled free of her braid and sprung like confused lightning bolts about her enchanting face.

"I'm not letting go," Ethan insisted.

"Fine with me, hot shot. But while you've been sprawled on your bed all day I've been lifting weights, so I'm pretty sure I can keep this up longer than you."

"What in blue blazes is going on in here?" Ben demanded loud enough to be heard over the dog's carrying on. His son's lazy body hitting the floor accounted for the loud noise, but the full explanation would be interesting. Actually, other than the manic hound, the scene was quite funny and the closest thing to rough-housing that he'd seen Ethan experience in years. Ben squashed down a grin and kept his distance from the action.

* * *

Ali gave a mighty yank, sufficient to pull Ethan a foot closer to the goal line she'd drawn on the rug with the toe of her favorite old ropers. The boy's long arms and legs were stretched end to end, looking like he was making a dive for the end zone. He'd aggravated her since she'd arrived, so this turnabout was not only fair play, it was fun.

Simba danced around his body, barking her pleasure.

"That's enough, girl," Ali quieted her beloved pet, then turned attention to the new arrival. "Sorry if we bothered you, Congressman. But I needed to score a point on this stubborn son of yours."

She tightened her grip and sucked in a breath. "Ethan seems to think nobody's the boss of him. Now, as his dad it's your call how to handle business between the two of you. But as his therapist, I'm the one callin' all the shots, no ifs, ands or buts."

"Real mature way to handle a kid, Ali." Trapped facedown during the struggle, Ethan's voice was muffled by the thick pile.

"That's *Doctor Stone*, to you." His father corrected.

"It's okay. We're on a first-name basis, aren't we, kiddo?" Ali gave another sharp tug and the boy's hands crossed the goal into her territory. "Sir, will you please verify the outcome of our tug-of-war?"

"Happy to accommodate." Long strides carried the former athlete across the floor, where he made note of Ethan's position compared to the faint line and nodded agreement. "By my calculations you are the winner."

One final yank for good measure and she flung her corner of the sheet over Ethan's head, hiding him from her view. She was fed up with the kid.

He flailed beneath the cover for a moment, then climbed to his feet, leaving the king-size square of fabric on the floor. He tossed his head like the ornery mule that he was and then stomped into his dressing room.

"Well, he got off the bed so I suppose today wasn't a total waste of time." She stooped to gather the sheet, then dropped it into the laundry hamper in the corner.

"So, what was that all about, Doctor Stone?"

"As I said, we're on a first-name basis and I'd appreciate it if you'd call me Ali."

"Then please, call me Ben."

"But you'd prefer Congressman Lamar, correct?"

Mixed emotions crossed his face, as if he wasn't sure how to answer. Or maybe he was deciding which of his responses a potential voter would rather hear.

"As appealing as it sounds to me, I don't know if that title will ever be mine." He ducked his head, suddenly shy.

The guy was a natural for politics. As handsome as West Texas is hot and with a humble act that would charm Attila the Hun. But Ali's strong suit was finding the kernel of truth among the lies her patients told, even to themselves, in order to cover their pain. Only Ali and God knew how many years she'd personally spent in denial, blocking out the horror of her childhood, choosing memories of abandonment over nightmares of abuse.

"Well, if you don't mind I'll use the powder room in the hall to freshen up and then meet you downstairs to explain the *progress* you just observed."

With the door closed behind her, Ali did a double take before the bathroom mirror.

"Good gravy, I look like I've just run a half-marathon."

She unthreaded the braid that had come loose in the struggle with Ethan, groped in her purse for a brush and made quick work of restoring her hair. A splash of water on hot cheeks and a good hand soaping completed her effort to regain some dignity but did little to improve her mood.

This ridiculous effort to get Ethan to groom himself had gone on for three days! The hours consumed by rituals, arguments and rationalizing on both sides were probably no sweat for a therapist who willingly lived on Planet Asperger. But Ali had made a private commitment to limit her counseling skills to abuse victims where she had a ton of personal knowledge.

But here she was anyway, dealing with this bizarre disorder again. It was giving her anxiety the likes of which she hadn't experienced since her earliest days in foster care. Ali's candle was melted at both ends from searching for wisdom. Between office sessions with her patients she pored over old research materials hoping for a long-forgotten clue. Then late into the night she surfed psychotherapy sites, reading updated studies on Asperger's hoping for a discovery.

And as she'd waited for Ethan to finish

today's diatribe on the chemical properties of sedimentary rock so he would finally get off the bed and change his sheets, only one thing was certain in her mind: she was ready to admit defeat.

"Ethan, I need to tell you something." Ali tried again to distract him. When he yammered on about salt and gypsum she used the time to gather what little was left of her paper-thin patience. If the attention he'd paid her over the past few days was any indicator, the boy probably wouldn't hear a word she said. So, why bother?

And that's when the fight broke out. Pillows flew, blankets were tossed and a battle for the linens became a life and death issue. But the bed *would* get stripped.

"After I drag you over this line, we're gone for good!"

"But you just got here," Ethan insisted between grunts of exertion. "Why are you leaving already?"

"For your information, bituminous breath," she jerked her head toward the clock placed prominently above his flat-screen television, "It's been two hours since I arrived and we haven't accomplished diddly squat."

"How can you say that?" Indignation filled his wide, incredulous eyes. "If you'd pay attention to me when I speak instead of constantly looking at your notes, you might learn something."

She ground her teeth, holding back the defensiveness that always accompanied being busted. She'd learned it was a waste of breath. The first time Ethan had called her out she'd been impressed with his intuitive nature. By the tenth time he'd taken her to task she realized he simply had no sense of tact. To an Aspie, diplomacy was tantamount to a lie. When something was straightforward, a candy coating made no sense. It was just that simple to Ethan, who had a remarkable ability to hit a nail on the head even if he could only hit one nail over and over and over again.

Enough already. Ali tossed her brush into her purse, resigned to what was about to happen. After the display of foolishness Benjamin Lamar had just witnessed, she didn't figure he'd want her coming back again anyway. She slung her bag over her shoulder, opened the door and headed down the stairs with Simba in tow.

Chapter Six

As Ali softly descended the staircase, her gaze came to rest on the wallmounted fountain above the massive fireplace. A cross, crafted from rusty and twisted barbed wire, was embedded in the burnished copper and gray slate sculpture. A sheet of living water tumbled down the slick surface of the stone, then bubbled across the barbs of the cross, whispering forgiveness.

There was movement near the windows, where she caught sight of Ethan's father. He was as lean as a Grecian statue and stood facing the twenty-foot wall of glass, with arms folded across his chest.

Probably searching for a positive way to say, "You're fired."

When her boots and Simba's feet tapped against the hardwood floor he turned his head. The broad smile on his face sent an unexpected sizzle through Ali's nervous system.

"Something funny?" Maybe he secretly enjoyed playing the bad guy once in a while.

"As a matter of fact, yes," he responded. "That whole scene upstairs was very funny. But I'm more pleased than amused."

"Pleased?" She dropped her purse on the sofa table, then pointed to a nearby throw rug where Simba settled comfortably with her head on her front paws. "How can you be pleased about wasting your money?"

"Excuse me?" He blinked, looking unsure of himself for the first time since they'd met.

He was in good company because Ali's self-confidence was shrinking by the minute. Ending this association sooner than later was probably for the best.

"My approach isn't working with Ethan so it's a waste of money to keep me involved in his treatment."

The heart-melting smile was back. "Let me be the judge of whether or not the return is worth the investment. Right now, I happen to think it is."

She slumped down on a plush floral sofa. He took the chair positioned at a right angle to the couch and propped his heels on the expensive-looking coffee table.

"Suppose you tell me what happened up there."

"Nothing happened, that's just it. I don't seem to be having any impact at all."

He shook his head. "That's where you're wrong. Give yourself time to get to know Ethan and you'll start to recognize what we call *progress* in this house. You got him to engage with you and it's only been a few days. That's more than I've accomplished in the past few weeks."

"I wouldn't normally call an argument that degenerated into a wrestling match an accomplishment," Ali countered.

"Tell me how your sessions usually play out." He slid lower in his oversized Queen Anne chair and folded large hands across his flat abdomen. Ali's head was splitting and she was ready to leave for the day, but he seemed to be settling in for a lengthy chat. She pressed fingertips to her temples and rubbed in small circles for a few moments before answering.

"Well, you have to remember that my

patients are all suffering from the effects of abuse. Their experience may have triggered some mental illness but nothing as profound as autism. So, with one of my usual clients, I lead them into discussions that will eventually allow us to deal with the root of their problem."

"Does that happen overnight?"

"Of course not." Ali knew she was being baited and it irked her already-agitated nerves. "Therapy is a time-consuming process that requires cooperation from everyone involved."

"Well, it's obvious we won't be getting much voluntary cooperation from my son anytime soon. But if you'd known Ethan before his Asperger's became unmanageable, you'd understand how desperate I am to give him every chance to regain some of the life he's lost. So while you may not be able to get his agreement, you will certainly have mine."

"Would you mind a personal question, Mr. Lamar?"

"Ben."

She opened her mouth but hesitated to speak his name.

"Is there another option? That just seems too casual for a man who could preside over

Congress one day. It would be like calling Governor Schwarzenegger 'Arnie.'"

Amused blue eyes rolled toward the ceiling. "You're getting the cart way before the horse. I'm not even in the race yet."

"Yet." She repeated, catching the tag.

"Back to my name," he sidestepped. "My sweet mama was the only person who ever called me Benjamin. I miss hearing it and I'd be honored if you'd use it." He didn't stray off subject but leaned forward, elbows on his knees. "Now, what's the question?"

His smile was intended to put her at ease. She hoped he wouldn't be upset with her for prying, but his answer was critical insight.

"How did Ethan get along with his mother?" Ali kept her voice soft and respectful.

Benjamin's eyes narrowed and his focus shifted to some point high on the wall for long moments as he considered what she'd asked.

"If it's too personal..." Ali prepared to apologize.

He sat tall in his chair and cleared his throat.

"Oh, it's not that," he insisted. "I was simply remembering how smitten Ethan was with his mama when he was a little boy. They couldn't get enough of each other. Then pre-adolescence came along and showing affection became awkward for him. By the time he hit puberty we were living with social anxiety symptoms we couldn't explain away.

"Ethan began to fall behind in classes and we started seeing signs of obsessive behavior. Then late one night he cut himself on the shin so deeply the bleeding wouldn't stop. He had to come to us for help. That's when we first saw the evidence that Ethan had been cutting for a while. He'd been careful to hide it under his clothing."

The story confirmed Ali's suspicion about the scars she'd noted on Ethan's leg the day of the rescue. She'd seen similar markings on the homeless kids she worked with on Sundays, their sick method of stress relief an external sign of the internal pain.

"Once we realized Ethan was self-injuring, Theresa gave up her interior design career and made it her mission to get our son a proper diagnosis and treatment. We'd known about the Asperger's for less than a year when my wife was killed. She lost control of her car during a heavy rainstorm and hit a tree. Ethan walked away without serious injury, but Theresa didn't make it through the night. He thinks he's somehow responsible and won't accept my forgiveness."

"It's more likely that he *can't* accept it," Ali corrected gently.

Benjamin shook his head. "My daddy used to say 'Cain't means won't.'"

The exaggerated drawl gave it a humorous matter-of-fact quality. Ali smiled at Benjamin sounding less polished and more country. More Texan. More appealing.

"Your daddy was a smart man, and in general terms I'd agree with him. But you mustn't overlook the fact that there are simply things Ethan's brain can't process. It stands to reason that if he's lacking the ability to do things that are second nature to most people, like tell a white lie, then he's probably lacking the ability to grieve. That's something you have to learn as you go through the experience. It sounds like Ethan's brain can't let the grief run its course. For most of us, when we eventually get to the end of sadness there's a sort of comfort in acceptance."

Benjamin seemed to consider what she'd said, then exhaled a loud sigh as he continued. "To answer your question, in the last months of her life Theresa was butting heads with him just like you did today. We had reasonable rules and expectations in our home, but it all flew out the window as he turned inward on himself. It's never gotten any better and I'm fresh out of wisdom."

The room was quiet for a while. Water trickled down the fountain above the fireplace and Simba rolled over on her side with a comfortable groan. Ali wanted nothing more than to curl up on the rug next to her friend, but she had to get home and enter everything she'd just learned into her computer notes. If she was still the therapist of record she needed to get to work.

Ali pushed to her feet and picked up her shoulder bag. Simba was at her side immediately, ready to follow. Benjamin stood as well, noted the sudden nearness of his four-legged nemesis and eased behind the safety of the big chair.

"For the most part she's a quiet dog," Ali tried to make Simba sound less threatening.

"With an animal that big and sneaky I'd actually prefer some barking. Silence means she could be lurking around any corner. Would you consider putting a bell on her collar when you come back next week?"

"So, you're *not* firing me?"

"Not a chance."

"Are you biting your nails again?" Erin demanded.

Ali yanked her hand away from her mouth and rested it on the steering wheel. How embarrassing to be busted long distance by her younger sibling.

"Ewww! Ali that is totally gross and not *even* worthy of my cell phone minutes!" The teen-speak Erin had picked up from her daughter made Ali's sister sound nothing like a thirty-four-year-old Pulitzer Prize-winning photojournalist.

"Don't hang up! I won't do it again," Ali pleaded. "I really need to talk to you."

"Okay, but I don't have long. Daniel and Dana are holding supper for me."

Alison smiled at the thought of Erin reconciled with her husband and daughter and living just up the road in Houston. It was actually over three hundred miles, but by Texas standards that was a hop, skip and a jump.

It had been a long journey back to family for Erin and Ali after being separated for almost twenty-five years. The immeasurable cost of their father's violent temper had included a brutal end to their mother's life, his ultimate death behind bars and the separation and estrangement of the three children. The sisters had only recently reconnected and their brother still refused to answer communications. But Ali was determined not to give up on reuniting what was left of their family.

In that regard she could relate to Benjamin, desperate to regain some of the life he and Ethan had lost.

"Back to the point of my call," she resumed the conversation. Now that her sister was on the line Ali wasn't so sure she wanted to blurt it all out. But if anybody could understand debilitating self-doubt, it was Erin. A woman who'd chased danger to prove to herself she wasn't a coward. "Remember the kid with Asperger's that I told you about?"

"Of course. Did his father do something else stupid?"

Ali winced, ashamed she'd given another person such a poor impression of a man she hardly knew herself. Yes, there was plenty about him she didn't agree with, but she was quickly coming to respect his dedication to Ethan.

"No, as a matter of fact he's not quite the bonehead I first thought."

"But you said his political support base included those crazies with the extreme parental rights platform. I searched the Internet on that bunch and they don't need a voice, they need handcuffs. I saw more liberal thinking among the Taliban."

Erin's years with World View News had afforded her a front-row seat to the international plight of children. She knew from personal experience there were worse things than foster care, and one of them was remaining in a dangerous home environment. But only Ali knew the true depth and damage of their father's depraved mind because she'd been the object of his sick *affection.*

"Has the guy commented on his platform to you?" Erin asked.

"So far we haven't had any reason to get into Benjamin's political affiliations."

"*Benjamin,* is it? Well, if we've become so familiar and he's not the *bonehead* you once thought, then what's the problem?" The connection crackled as Erin waited on her sister's reply.

"The problem is me."

"Well, that's pretty specific. Could you be a little more general?"

"Erin Elise, I'm not up to this kid." Ali reached for the a/c, switched it on high and pointed the vent at her face. "The short circuits in his brain are impossible to anticipate. One moment you think you're speaking with a bright, fifteen-year-old boy and the next he's looking at you like you've just sprouted horns. His communication skills have gone haywire."

"For example?"

"Ethan doesn't understand that the rest of the world is not enamored of igneous rock the way he is."

"That doesn't sound so awful," Erin cajoled.

"And it's not for the first thirty minutes the initial time he gives his lecture. But he goes on and on and on, endlessly. No amount of yawning or looking at my watch or fidgeting gets through to him."

"I get that he's boring and self-absorbed. What else?"

"His hygiene is deplorable. The boy could care less whether or not he bathes or changes his clothes."

"I hear ya, he's lazy. What else?"

"Even the smallest verbal exchange becomes

a dispute. Ethan won't answer a simple question without making it contentious. He's a one-man debate team."

"Okay, let me make sure I've got this straight. The kid is wrapped up in his own world and couldn't care less about what you think, he'd rather lie on the bed than make it up and he challenges your every word."

"Exactly!" Ali was getting worked up just discussing it with Erin. But it felt good to know she understood.

"Big sister, surely you don't need me to tell you that Asperger's or not, most teenagers behave just like that."

"Yes, but you eventually get through to them, and you can make a difference in their lives!" Ali's voice rose so much that Simba's head popped up, her floppy ears alert for sounds of trouble. There was silence on the other end of the line as she waited on her sister's response.

Ali felt the pressure of deeply buried emotions well up in her throat, knowing there was so much more to the story.

Chapter Seven

"Ali, what's this *really* all about?" Erin asked. "You're very good at your job and you know it takes time and patience to change behavior. Why the big rush to throw in the towel on this case?"

Ali steered the Land Rover into a nearby Waffle House parking lot and slipped between the lines of an empty space. She lowered the windows and cut the engine, glad it was late and nobody would see her so close to tears. She crossed her right forearm over her eyes to block out a nearby street lamp.

"Ali, you still there?"

"Yes," she whispered into the cell phone.

"Hey! I can hear how upset you are. Talk to me."

Talk was good therapy Ali knew that for a

fact. But she also knew there were some memories better left undisturbed. She'd try to explain this to Erin but there were not enough words in the English language to describe how she'd felt when that call had come in late one night nearly eight years ago.

"Doctor Stone? This is Rose from your answering service. Darien Sims was pronounced dead on arrival at City General about two hours ago. His mother found his body when she made her nightly check on him. Darien had hung himself in his closet."

Ali was stunned by the news, unable to speak.

"Doctor Stone? I hope I did the right thing by calling you so late."

"Of course you did, Rose. Good night."

Ali tried to stand but her legs folded beneath her. Instead of climbing to her feet she only made it as far as her knees, where she wept and prayed for the soul of the boy everyone had failed.

The boy with Asperger's.

"Oh, Ali, I had no idea," Erin's voice was hushed.

"They taught us in school that patient suicide was a professional hazard nobody escapes. But being armed with that fact in your head doesn't prepare you to deal with it in your heart." She crossed her arms and hugged her chest where it ached with the memory. "It seems like young people today are more desperate to get away from their problems than we ever were. Even in my darkest days I never considered taking my life to escape what I was enduring."

"You don't feel responsible for that boy's death, do you?"

"No." Ali shook her head, a reassuring motion. "But I can't help thinking that I treated his case like a lab exercise instead of the life of a human being."

"What do you mean?"

"For my Ph.D. dissertation I chose Asperger's and studied Darien's case for months. It wasn't until Darien took his own life that I realized I'd never fully engaged with him. I had no idea he was capable of carrying out the act of suicide."

"And you believed you'd failed him?"

"Of course. But even worse, I felt justified in keeping my distance. If I don't keep an emotional-free zone with my clients my spirit will be like an open wound that never heals." Ali was afraid that revealing her self-centered nature would drive away the sister she hardly knew as an adult.

"Ali, I understand. Really, I do." Erin's voice

was soft, forgiving as she spoke into her phone. "I built a career out of observing and documenting other people's lives. And I knew all along exactly what it was—a vicarious existence without the messy personal part."

"Do you feel like you missed out on real life?"

"Oh, sure. But Dana and Daniel are giving me a crash course and it's a wild ride." Erin chuckled.

"Well, enjoy this special time, Erin Elise. You deserve good things."

"That's true for both of us, Ali. The Lord is using you in a powerful way, so don't be too hard on yourself."

Ali lowered her chin and mouthed *"Thank You,"* eternally grateful that Erin was a believer.

"You're pretty smart, you know that?" Ali complimented Erin. "You've given your favorite sister some good advice. Got any for your favorite therapist?"

Erin snapped her fingers near the phone as if she'd just had a light-bulb moment.

"As a matter of fact, I might. One of the ways I got Dana to let down her defenses and just be herself was over pizza and Scrabble."

"You know, it may take all night, but it's worth a try."

"Better keep him away from those red triple-word squares and get the latest version of Webster's."

"Yeah, this kid could do some damage with stuff like 'metamorphosis' and 'geochronology' in his vocabulary."

The conversation ended on a humorous note as Erin headed off to be with her family and Ali pointed the Land Rover toward home. Her exhaustion and aggravation were forgotten as she tried to remember where she'd last seen the big, fat dictionary she'd used in college to prop up a thrift store sofa that was missing one leg.

"What on earth is she doing here on the weekend?" Ben muttered to himself, surprisingly pleased when the big tires of Ali's SUV crunched on his driveway. Maybe she'd left something behind during her visit the night before. Or maybe his home was simply where she wanted to be on a Saturday evening. Yeah, right.

From his position at the stovetop Ben could make out the boxy vehicle through the slatted shutters on the kitchen window. The tailgate slammed as she undoubtedly released her shadow. Ben continued to whisk the sauce in the iron skillet while waiting for the doorbell. After several more minutes he poured the fragrant gravy over the seared pork loin and returned the mouth-watering dish to a hot oven.

With Mrs. Alvarez still on vacation Ben was practicing one of the recipes he'd learned from many hours of watching the Food Network. It seemed to be the only cable channel where he could be certain the celebrities would keep clothes on their bodies and a pleasant tongue in their mouths.

Ben glanced toward the breakfast nook where he'd set one place for himself and added a mason jar filled with fresh flowers from the back yard. He had to eat alone, but there was no reason he couldn't be civilized. He dried his hands on a dish towel, then slung it over his shoulder. Opening the window shutter gave him full view of the front drive and yard.

"Where'd they go?" He craned his neck but didn't see any sign of the pretty redhead or her dog. He moved to the back of the kitchen, glanced out the bay window and spotted the pair. Their backs were to him as they walked the depth of the property.

It was still natural for him to compare all women to his late wife who'd been a classic, willowy blonde. Alison Stone couldn't have been more different and he was glad of it. It was odd enough having a female visit his home on a weekend, let alone a number of days in a row. If she'd borne any resemblance at all to Theresa it might have been difficult. But Ali was unique with her auburn twist of hair trailing down a rounded backside that was dressed once again in blazes of colorful cotton, denim and Southwestern silver. Her blue jean skirt grazed the top of her western boots as she walked. Polished conchos on her belt glinted in the afternoon sun.

Ben stepped away from the window before Ali had a chance to turn and catch him staring. He opened several cans, dumped the contents into a large bowl along with eggs and spices and then whipped the mixture vigorously as he launched into his usual, one-sided conversation.

Lord, give me something to work with here, some encouragement in one direction or the other. I need more than my worry for Ethan to occupy my life. If I'm not going to be campaigning, then I'd like to get back on the speaking circuit. But if I can't even coax my son out of his room, why would anybody pay me to teach them the principles of positive thinking?

With the pie filling prepared, Ben turned his attention to the homemade crust that waited on a dusting of flour over the cool, granite counter. Following Paula Deen's example, he scooped up the pastry, positioned it in a deep baking dish, then began to crimp the edges. As he pinched the dough, he continued his words with God.

It just seemed like common sense to me that Ethan would be in hog heaven surrounded by all those incredible rock formations in Big Bend. Nobody ever appreciated Your sculpting skills more than that kid. I'm not surprised he slipped out to get a closer look, but I didn't expect him to feel like he'd been abandoned. Father, how could I have misjudged this so completely and undone all the good we'd accomplished up to that point? Show me a sign that we'll get back on track and move forward with our lives again.

The chimes above the front door echoed in the entry hall. Alison Stone. Ben glanced upward.

And please, please don't let that be the sign, Lord.

Ben shook the excess flour off his hands and stepped to the edge of the kitchen.

"Ali?"

"Guilty."

"It's unlocked."

The door inched open. "Benjamin?" she called, evidently reluctant to let herself in.

He appreciated that.

"In the kitchen." He shouted above water running in the sink. "Sorry for being so informal, but I didn't want to keep you waiting on the step while I washed up."

"Good afternoon," she greeted him.

Ben dried his hands. As he turned toward Ali's pleasant smile he struggled not to do a double take. She'd been so lovely from a distance, but that was usually an optical illusion, right? Didn't everybody look better from fifty yards? But now, standing five feet away she was a vision.

She twitched her nose and sniffed the air, drawn as if against her will to the top half of the oven. "What smells so wonderful?"

"It's not much, just a pork loin in au jus and some roasted vegetables," he exaggerated modesty. "A little something I threw together after a week of nonstop cooking shows." He tipped the bowl of filling into his pie shell.

"A true Renaissance man." She sounded impressed.

He waved away her praise with the spatula

he'd used to scrape the bowl. "No, just a really hungry man who hates to eat alone. There's going to be plenty if you'd like to join me later. The meat still needs to roast for a while."

"Oh, no, I hadn't intended to invite myself to dinner on a Saturday evening."

"Now that you mention it—" he held up his hands in a *what gives* gesture "—shouldn't you be out with your steady guy on Saturday night?"

She shook her head. "God's never put the right man in my life. And at thirty-seven I'm starting to think that's not part of the plan. Right now it's okay because I work seven days a week with my kids."

Ben opened the bottom oven, slid the pie inside and set the timer. "That's how it was with me and football. I wasn't around much when Ethan was a baby."

"Speaking of Ethan…" Ali produced the box that had been tucked beneath her arm. The contents rattled as she presented it, her expression hopeful.

"Scrabble?" Ben read the title. "Gosh, I haven't played that in thirty years."

"I thought I'd give it a try. Maybe he'll go for it."

"There's only one way to find out. He's upstairs, like always."

She stopped at the doorway. "Aren't you going to ask me where Simba is?"

"I'm sure she's just around that corner, close enough to be at my throat in a moment's notice."

"Oh, I thought maybe I'd fooled you into thinking I'd left her at my place."

He shook his head. "Nope, I saw you both out back earlier."

She lowered her gaze, seemingly embarrassed. "I'm sorry we didn't ask permission. But we're kinda pressed for space at the condo, especially since I took in a roommate. I just couldn't resist a look around your yard. It seems huge compared to our little public park, and your landscaping is extraordinary. I hoped you wouldn't mind strangers wandering on your property."

"Don't mention it. You're hardly a stranger, so feel free to make yourself at home."

He had a feeling it was what she'd do anyway.

Chapter Eight

"Anybody home?" Ali knocked briskly on the door frame before entering Ethan's room. As expected, he was propped against his headboard with an ancient geology textbook in one hand and a Snickers bar in the other.

"What are you doing here?"

"It's always a pleasure to see you too, Ethan."

Ali dragged a side chair across the floor and positioned it at the Danish modern partner's desk. Then she unfolded the game board and set out a small wooden rack for each player. Ethan shifted from his backside to his knees so he could see what was going on. Good, she had his attention.

"Don't you know it's the weekend?" he snapped.

"So?" She began flipping the letter tiles facedown in the lid of the box. "If you never leave your room how can you tell today's any different from yesterday?"

"Morning cartoons, Sherlock."

"Very nice. You actually made a wisecrack."

"What do you mean by that?"

"It's not important." A teenager who didn't naturally dole out sarcasm wasn't necessarily a bad thing. "To your point, I'm definitely aware it's Saturday evening and I felt like doing something fun. I thought you might be interested in a Scrabble smackdown."

"That's a stupid kid's game."

"Oh, is that right?" Benjamin crossed the threshold carrying an additional chair. "In that case you probably won't want to join us."

"Of course he will." Ali suppressed her shock and continued to set up the game. Inviting Benjamin to play had crossed her mind but she'd dismissed it after a moment's thought. Working with Ethan was like groping about in a dark and unfamiliar closet. If she was going to fumble blindly it was best to do it in private.

"How about it, Ethan?" Ali kept her voice casual.

"Nope." He slumped back onto the bed but continued to watch, incapable of masking the interest on his face.

"Alrighty, then." She turned to Benjamin, who winked and grinned at her as he passed the foot of Ethan's bed. Another woman might have interpreted the gesture as flirtatious, but Ali felt certain it was conspiratorial and nothing more. Even so, such a teasing glance from the Dallas Cowboy legend was the stuff that drove Bridget Jones to her diary.

"I'm glad you have some time to kill before your dinner's ready."

"Pffffff," Benjamin puffed at the comment. "If a rousing round of Scrabble is in order, the food can wait."

The game was positioned between the two of them with the board only partially in Ethan's line of sight. Ali prayed his curious nature would get the best of him and it took less than fifteen minutes to receive her answer.

"Huh?" Ali squinted at the word Benjamin had carefully positioned on the board. "Anth…Anthr…I can't even pronounce that. You're making it up," she accused him as she grabbed her trusty dictionary.

"No way," Benjamin defended himself.

"Way!" She thumbed through the pages. "A-N-T... How'd you spell that, again?"

"A-N-T-H-R-A-C-I-T-E."

"Anthracite!" Ethan was on his feet and crossing the room. "That's the most highly metamorphosed form of coal, containing ninety-two to ninety-eight percent of fixed carbon. It is black, hard and glassy." He selected a dark chunk from the many cylinder-shaped core samples on his bookshelves, carried it to the desk and positioned it beside the word on the Scrabble board. "Any dummy knows about Anthracite."

"Well, that certainly accounts for you," Ali muttered.

"Okay, you two. Keep it civil." Benjamin never looked up, just reached for more letter tiles to replenish the ones he'd used during his turn.

So, she'd been right not to swat his hand when he'd nonchalantly rifled around in the box for those Ts and As. He was up to something and Ali didn't know whether to feel relieved or challenged.

Who's the therapist here, anyway?

Benjamin made a show of adding up his score. "That's fifteen points for the old man." He wrote it on the pad with a flourish.

Ethan reached around his father's shoulder, scooted the H aside and pointed out the pink square underneath.

"Dad, pay attention. That's a double-word space."

"So it is! Thanks, buddy." Benjamin erased and re-entered his score.

"Hey, no assistance from the cheap seats." Ali waved Ethan away.

"She's right, son. Either pull up a chair and play or go back to bed, but don't loom over us like Mount Rushmore."

Ali watched for the boy's response. His eyes glazed with confusion, like a dog caught in the middle of a busy road, not knowing whether to freeze on the spot or run for the safety of the curb. Instinct told her to intervene.

"Here, take my seat and see if you can do anything with these crummy letters I drew." She stood and indicated the chair. When he continued to hesitate she walked around the desk, pinched the hem of his T-shirt and tugged Ethan forward. "Really, I could use the help. I'm much better at Monopoly but this was the only game in my closet that still had all the pieces."

Ethan slumped down, shoved both hands

through the mop of hair sticking outward from his scalp and held that pose while he studied the tray containing seven letter tiles.

Benjamin's head popped up from where he'd been concentrating on his next move.

"I think I smell something burning." He jumped to his feet. "Ali, would you mind taking my turn while I check on the pie?" Without waiting for her response or Ethan's objection, Benjamin headed out the doorway. A moment later his head poked back into the room. "And no cheating," he admonished, then hurried to the end of the hall and thumped down the staircase.

"I interfered upstairs, and I'm sorry for doing that without your permission." Benjamin's apology flowed the moment Ali appeared in the kitchen a couple of hours later.

She didn't bother pretending she had no idea what he meant. "Yes, you did meddle in my business but it worked out well, so you're forgiven." And she had to admit, if only to herself, it had been heartwarming to watch his devious efforts to engage Ethan in the game.

"I warn you, it probably won't be the last time," Benjamin admitted.

"That's okay, because I have every intention of sticking my nose into your professional affairs the first chance I get."

"I held off on supper, hoping you'd join me. There hasn't been a lady at my table in a long time, so my hosting skills are sorta rusty." He waved a hand toward the bay window where he'd positioned a second place setting at the banquette. "If you'd prefer something more formal, we can move into the dining room."

"Gosh, no. I wouldn't know formal if it jumped up and bit me." She walked to the table and counted the number of forks beside each plate. Four.

"Anything wrong?" he asked.

"If this is what you consider informal, I'd hate to see how much silver it takes to feed you by candlelight."

Benjamin rested a fist at either side of his waist and stared at the table, considering his efforts.

"Cocktail, salad, dinner, dessert." He pointed as he explained.

"This is a lovely kitchen, but it is not the Ritz Carlton. One fork will do, two tops."

"You think?"

"Definitely."

After nodding agreement he swept several utensils away from the table, dropped them into an open utility drawer and then placed a meal before them that Ali couldn't have cooked on a dare. During Benjamin's blessing her stomach rumbled like a diesel engine. She risked a peek and caught him smiling as he prayed. The more she knew of him the less by-the-book and more approachable he seemed.

He dished up man-sized portions of fragrant roasted meat, tender vegetables and bubbling gravy. Butter trickled from a crisp, warm roll. If she ate everything on the plate, she'd be too full for dessert. Oh, well. Maybe she'd be crude and ask for her slice of pie to go.

"So tell me, how many more words actually ended up on that board after I left the two of you alone?"

"Very few, seeing as neither of us hand-picked our letters and Ethan refused to stoop to any word with a score under ten points." She placed a heaping forkful into her mouth and groaned approval as she chewed.

"Thank you." He smiled at her reaction. "It's nice to have another person appreciate my efforts."

"I'm certain there are thousands of people who'll appreciate your efforts once you're a Congressman."

"You keep bringing that up. May I assume your interest means you'd support me?" He kept his eyes lowered to his plate. Ali couldn't tell if that was to keep the pressure off her or to mask his level of concern for the response.

"Honestly?" It was time to find out how much of this man was tough guy, how much was positive spin doctor and how much was ego.

This time his blue eyes met and held her gaze. "Of course. I'd like to know if you'd vote for me."

"Unfortunately, after what I've learned about one of your potential political action committees, the answer is no. A vote for you would be a vote for that group of crazies."

His chin snapped up as if he'd been popped in the jaw.

"Wow, I haven't been zinged like that since you called me an unconscionable idiot."

"Does this shoe fit as well as that one did?"

"Lady, you are a pit bull."

"I've been called worse." But never by anyone as high on the Texas social register as Benjamin Lamar.

"Suppose you tell me exactly which group of *'crazies'* you're referring to."

He opened the window of opportunity. Should she back down now?

Hmmmmm… No.

"The Parents First Alliance."

"The PFA is a strong source of support to the autism community. What do you have against their work?"

"Nothing where autism is concerned. But do you realize how often they challenge Family Services for removing children from dangerous homes?"

"As a matter of fact, I do. I happen to agree with them that children are better off with their natural parents than they are in the court system."

"Have you studied that subject?"

"I've read all the literature PFA provided to me."

"Those marketing materials are tantamount to propaganda. Have you studied this subject *personally?* Have you spoken with enough victims of domestic violence to find out that most of them would feel safer living under a viaduct than trapped in a house with a drunken mother or raging father?" She rested her fork on the edge of the plate, the tempting food forgotten as she thought of her young friends, her Sunday Kids, who'd go hungry tonight before they'd go home.

"No, I haven't." He stared as if studying her face.

"Well, I work with some of those kids during my personal time. There's an epidemic of teens on the streets who've taken matters into their own hands when people like Parents First Alliance let them down."

She was being too blunt, but he'd asked for honesty.

"Benjamin, a couple of years ago the PFA financed the defense of that cult compound where there were clearly signs of child abuse. A man would have to be ignorant or a gullible fool to support their agenda."

The lady's words carried the unexpected sting of a scorpion hiding in the toe of a sock. Ben couldn't remember ever being confronted so aggressively off the field of competition and certainly never in his own home. He counted to ten, determined to remain calm, resolved not to react like one of the *'crazies'* she'd just accused him of associating with.

This woman obviously knew her subject

matter and she wasn't afraid to bring the heat. Should he compliment her on a thorough investigation of the facts or escort her out of his house for insulting his integrity?

And either way, what if she was right?

Chapter Nine

Ben would take this up with God later, but right now the woman across the table had made some comments that had to be addressed.

Randy Mason had arranged their initial meeting with the reps for Parents First Alliance. Trusting Randy with his life, Ben naturally assumed these folks who'd given generously to autism research were completely on the up and up. Yes, there'd been some negative press during their court battles to keep kids out of the system and under the guardianship of their parents, but wasn't that what parental rights were all about?

Had he been naïve to trust Randy's judgment without question? Probably, since Ben was now questioning himself while the lady at his kitchen table waited, staring, expecting a rebuttal.

"I'd like to answer your concerns, but you have me at a disadvantage. I need to do more research on the PFA and their legal battles with Child Protective Services."

"With all due respect, you should have done due diligence on that subject *before* you decided to associate with the PFA."

Fed up with the attack, Ben mirrored her actions, laying down his fork and pushing back from his plate.

"You know what, Doctor Stone? Until further notice I'm still a private citizen. Who I associate with is really none of your business. However, you've scored some points and given me plenty to think about. For that I thank you. Once I've declared myself a political candidate you're welcome to get in line with the opposition and have at me. But I'll also thank you to keep your thoughts on my personal affiliations to yourself, at least in my home and certainly with my son."

Ben's defensive words rebounded in the vaulted ceiling above the kitchen and then the room fell silent. If there'd been a cricket in the house, they'd have heard it chirping. At this moment he'd even welcome the tapping of the dog's nails on the floor nearby as an excuse to break eye contact with Alison Stone. She blinked first, pushed her chair back from his table and placed the folded napkin beside her plate.

"I'll see myself out," she said quietly.

"You don't have to leave." His mama would be horrified. His unkind words were about to run this woman out the door.

"It's getting late anyway, so I think it would be best." She crossed to the built-in desk where she'd set her bag, fished inside it and pulled out a ring of keys.

"Would you at least take your dinner with you?" Ben offered, knowing he had too much food and no appetite to continue the meal or the conversation.

"No thanks. I have leftover pizza."

If he wanted this to be the last he saw of Doctor Alison Stone here was the perfect opportunity to say so.

But in spite of her spitfire personality, he really liked the lady.

And what about Ethan?

"Should we expect a visit from you tomorrow?" Ben probed.

"My Sundays are reserved for worship and personal time with some of those young people I was telling you about."

"Let me rephrase. Should we expect a visit from you ever again?"

Her shoulders drooped for a moment as if the weight of the question were too great. Then, she looked him right in the eye. "Mr. Lamar, I've never run from a problem or a challenge. I know I had my doubts about working with Ethan, but as of today I consider him one of my kids. I try never to let them down because everybody deserves to have at least one person they can count on to accept them unconditionally."

She turned about face, not giving Ben the opportunity to remind her that Ethan had plenty of people he could count on. The heels of her boots thunked loudly across the tile floor and then more quietly on the wood of the entry hall. The alarm system chirped as the door opened and closed behind the very opinionated woman.

Ben stared at her plate and the food that would go to waste now. She'd only enjoyed a few bites before their pleasant mealtime conversation had gone south. How had that happened, anyway? She'd transitioned rather quickly from complimenting his cooking to sniping at his supporters. Could she be down on politics in general or was there a reason she'd drawn a bead on his campaign in particular?

The rumble of her SUV brought him to his feet. Ben crossed the kitchen to peer through the window shutters. The backs of two heads were visible through the windshield above the tailgate. The head with long, floppy ears turned toward the house just as the vehicle exited Ben's driveway. He would have bet dollars to donuts he was being stared down by that blasted dog.

Simba whined.

Ali checked the rearview mirror and noticed her pet looking backward, toward the house.

"I know, girl. You're tired of spending your evenings back there lying on a rug when we should be getting ready for the Round Up."

Volunteer rescue workers came from across the Southwest each summer for their very own faceoff. The full morning of climbing, rappelling and confronting obstacles determined the best of the best in ability and preparedness. And when it came to master and canine teams, Ali and Simba were the gold standard. The two excelled in the competition, working as one against the clock, moving together instinctively. They did it for fun—the glory was just gravy.

Gravy.

Her stomach grumbled. Pizza again. Yuck.

"I should have taken him up on that offer of a to-go plate."

As Ali began the long drive back into town she acknowledged feelings of regret for some of what she'd said. It was too soon to be so blunt. She hadn't given him a chance, been too judgmental. She'd accused the popular motivational speaker of being gullible, for heaven's sake!

"Wait a minute. There was nothing wrong with what I said," Ali tried to convince herself. "But there was nothing right about it, either," she gave equal time to her conscience.

Simba whined again, still watching the road behind them.

"I thought you didn't like him."

Eyes like Moon Pies stared from the folding wire travel crate in the rear of the SUV.

"Okay, I'll call and apologize." Ali kept her gaze on the road. She reached for her bag in the front passenger seat. Nothing. She glanced to her right. The space where her handbag should be sitting was empty.

Oh, nice.

Pressing the brake, she pulled to the side of

the road while she counted all the valid reasons for going back. Then she examined the only argument she could come up with for waiting until Monday. The fine for driving without a license beat her pride by a mile. She whipped the Land Rover into a lefthand U-turn, wishing she was headed back to the three-story mansion to eat pork instead of crow.

"I'll keep it short and sweet. Just offer a quick apology, grab my purse and get the blazes out of Dodge."

She cut the headlights and swung into the wide, circular driveway. The main level was dark except for a chandelier glowing inside the foyer, above the doorway.

She'd been gone about fifteen minutes, just long enough for the sun to set. Had Benjamin already managed to clean the kitchen and lock up for the night? The man was annoyingly efficient. Clearly, he wasn't that thorough about everything since he knew so little about his financial backers.

"Enough already," she warned herself. With the windows down on such a pleasant evening Simba was safe and comfortable inside the Rover.

Instead of making a beeline for the front

walk, Ali veered to the side of the magnificent home where the west-facing overlook beckoned. Three steps up and she stood atop the flagstone surface that had been positioned for a perfect glimpse of the horizon. The sky was dark, dark blue with only a thin line of red-orange above the earth, a shallow puddle of color left by the sun.

Security lights had sprung to life in the gardens below, casting long shadows beside the topiary and poolside cabana. In the far corner where she and Simba had walked earlier, Benjamin sat on a concrete bench beneath a decorative lamppost.

All alone.

Ali's heart thumped, a combination of guilt and pain. And something else she didn't want to accept. It ached for the man, surrounded by the trappings of success with nothing but memories of his personal loss for company.

"Lord, help me out here," she whispered. *"He deserves the same compassion I give my Sunday Kids. And instead of showing the love of Christ I treat him like he's guilty of a crime."*

Benjamin stood and moved toward the house with shoulders hunched forward, and hands shoved deep into the pockets of his khaki slacks. He looked so much like his son upstairs, who lacked the ability to recognize help or accept forgiveness.

She should kick herself. When it came right down to it, all Benjamin wanted to do was serve the public and be a good role model. Not really much different from football or all that positive guru business.

Not really much different from a therapist "who donates more time than she bills," Ali's roommate was fond of pointing out. Josie, the nursing student Ali had taken into her home, helped in the office to cover her rent. Each month she reminded her boss that patient gratitude was not an acceptable form of payment for Ali's mountain of student loans.

Simba woofed lightly. She was restless to be going.

"Just get it over with," Ali reminded herself of the reason she was trespassing in the dark instead of cozy in front of her television with Josie and her snoring cat. Ali crossed to the front door and rang the bell. Several moments later the porch light blazed and the door swung open.

The good lookin' man before her was still every inch a fearsome linebacker. Except, of course, for the purse. He stood in the foyer with both strong arms extended. A paper plate covered in foil was balanced on one hand and her bag dangled from the other.

"Nice accessorizing." She was glad for something silly to say.

"Thank you." He turned it this way and that, checking it out. "It's my favorite designer knockoff."

She pretended to squint disapproval and then snatched the strap from his hand.

"What took you so long to come back?" His lips were pressed together in a meager effort not to grin.

"I had to think it over for a few miles before I was ready to call and apologize."

He shook his head. "No apology is necessary if you meant what you said."

"Well, I did mean it, but I should have found a less confrontational way to express myself. Life has been a series of battles since I was about eight years old, so it's second nature for me to be on the offensive."

"I'm up to it. My reputation with the Cowboys was built on being the best at defensive play. I held my ground against guys as unstoppable as runaway freight trains. I ought to be able to handle anything a beautiful woman can dish out, so bring it on."

She waved goodbye as she fanned away his challenge, then turned and headed for the Rover before the blush rushing up the column of her throat was visible beneath the home security lights. Once she was safely inside the vehicle she let the force of his words flow over her.

He called me beautiful! Benjamin Lamar thinks I'm beautiful!

As the silly old maid thought resounded in Ali's mind, she mentally ground it beneath the heel of her boot, determined not to be distracted by empty flattery. He was a politician. What female could ever be sure this man's compliments were real? A woman shouldn't let her head be turned by charming words—not if she was smart.

There would be strings attached as long as he was looking for a vote. But how nice it might be to become entangled in those strings!

Chapter Ten

Ben muted the Monday evening news while he considered his daily conversation with Randy. It hadn't gone well. Being an experienced lawyer, Randy quickly recognized Ben's questions for what they were: a cross-examination. Things started out friendly enough, but when Ben insisted on funding a third-party review of all political action committees who'd expressed interest in supporting his Congressional bid, Randy's back went up like a black cat's on Friday the thirteenth.

"Did you fall on your head over the weekend, my friend? You know I'd rather kiss a rattlesnake on the lips than give somebody our hard-earned money just for their opinion," Randy objected.

It wasn't worth getting into an argument. There was plenty more for Randy to manage, so Ben would handle this himself. After all, it would be his name on the ballot. In that regard Ali had been one hundred percent correct. It was up to Ben to ensure every alliance he made was credible and in line with his values.

And while he did believe children were ultimately better off with the family than placed in foster care, something Ali said had haunted him all weekend.

Life has been a series of battles since I was about eight years old.

Did Ali know firsthand about living in a dangerous home? His gut told him survival might be the key to her strength.

He'd missed the presence of the unpredictable lady on Sunday. Wished she'd stopped by yesterday so they could get to know each other better.

The mantle clock chimed seven times. She was later than usual. But then Ben really didn't know what *usual* meant for an attractive single woman with the demanding career and volunteer responsibilities she shouldered. She'd shown amazing courage and insight in taking him to task on Saturday night. Ben suspected there was a lot he could learn from Ali if he could get her to slow down and answer more questions than she asked.

A door slammed in the driveway.

"The lady and I must be on the same wavelength," Ben muttered through a pleased grin. He pushed up and out of his recliner, clicked off the television and tossed the remote on the end table.

"I hope you brought Yahtzee tonight but I'll settle for another game of Scrabble," he teased loudly as he yanked the door open.

"I told you our candidate had a sense of humor." Randy stood on the doorstep accompanied by a tall, white-haired gentleman Ben didn't recognize.

"Hey, buddy." Ben reached for his friend and pulled him into a brotherly embrace. "I wasn't expecting you."

"Evidently. But I'm pretty fair at Scrabble if that offer still stands."

"Ben Lamar, welcome to my home." He extended his hand to the stranger, then waited for an introduction.

"Sanders Boyd." The man's handshake was unnecessarily firm.

Another guy who thinks crushing my fingers will impress a former NFL player.

"Ben," Randy explained, "Sanders is the founder of the Parents First Alliance. I called to set up a meeting for later in the week, found out he was free and took a chance that you might be able to give us a few minutes tonight."

"Sure, I can always spare some time to talk shop."

Over their shoulders Ben watched Ali's SUV whip into the drive. God's timing proved He had a wry sense of humor. Ben needed to get Ali past these guys and upstairs to Ethan. If introductions were made all around, there was a good chance an altercation, if not a full-blown incident, would break out.

Her scuffed ropers clipped a determined path for the front door but Simba strayed toward the grass. Ben stepped aside and wasted no time ushering Sanders into the house, then turned to Randy.

"Why don't you take Mr. Boyd into my study and as soon as I have a word with Dr. Stone I'll join you."

Randy nodded. But after one step across the threshold he balked, turned back. "Wait a minute. *The* Dr. Stone? The woman who rescued Ethan?"

"I made the pickup but the rescue is always

a team effort," Ali said modestly as she approached. She seemed worn out, as usual.

Ben had come to accept Ali's harried look as part of the very unique package—boots in need of polish, collar smashed beneath her shoulder strap and silky strands of red hair pulling free of her braid. Even so, her one-of-a kind beauty rocked him back on his heels with each encounter.

Randy's expression filled with questions. He cleared his throat and looked expectantly at Ben. There was no civilized way out. May as well get it over with.

"Doctor Alison Stone, I'd like to introduce my old friend Randy Mason." As the two exchanged greetings Ben exaggerated a stage whisper. "Don't get too chummy with this guy. He'll get *lawyer* on you." The joke only provided a brief chuckle, then Ben was forced to continue, especially since Boyd had rejoined them on the front step.

"Ali, this is Sanders Boyd. He and Randy just dropped by for an impromptu meeting so feel free to go on upstairs. Ethan's expecting you and you're in for a nice surprise."

Ben made the last part up. He'd apologize profusely to God and Ali later.

As Boyd extended his hand Ben watched her normally pleasant expression morph into contempt. Not good.

"Mr. Sanders and I have met," she acknowledged, refusing to accept his handshake.

Though she kept her eyes on Boyd, Ben felt himself locked in the heat of her peripheral vision. If he so much as squirmed, she'd pounce like a starving dog on a bone. And speaking of dogs, hers sidled up and took a seat. Could things possibly get more uncomfortable?

"I'm sorry?" Boyd seemed puzzled.

"It was in a courtroom two years ago."

Yep, there was plenty of discomfort to go around.

Boyd waited for more detail. Clearly he could not recall the meeting.

"Surely you remember twelve-year-old Jason Maxwell. He'd been removed from the family home by Child Protective Services."

Boyd nodded. "Ah, yes. And I believe the court found in favor of the parents and returned the boy to their custody."

"Yes, that's right. And do you know what became of Jason?"

"I presume he's a high school student by now."

Ali's smile was brittle, not at all genuine.

"I guess you could say that. He's in the Texas Department of Corrections' secondary education program. Jason's serving twenty-to-life for the murder of his father. I visit him regularly, that is if he's not on suicide lockdown."

Sanders Boyd's spine stiffened. "And your point, young lady?"

Ali sighed and closed her eyelids, clearly exasperated with the man's feigned innocence. When she raised her gaze it was focused on Ben.

"This is your home. Do I have your permission to go there or would you prefer I ignore the question?"

"You don't need my permission, Ali. Say what's on your mind." Ben meant it. If a fight broke out, he'd just step aside and let Simba handle it.

Ali's amber eyes flecked with gold fixed on Boyd. The crimson glow that had been creeping up her neck reached her jaw and shot through her cheeks. The passion she felt for the subject was undeniable. But Boyd showed little emotion. In fact, a self-satisfied expression fixed on his pale face like a silent challenge. Ben would have given in to the desire to laugh if he hadn't known the Rock was about to crash down on the old man's arrogant head.

Ali's voice was steady when she spoke. "My point, sir, is that protecting parental rights is not the same as protecting the child."

"The system is broken," Boyd insisted. "We have to take a stand for the family."

"But the consequences, Mr. Boyd, fall on the lives of the children."

"Doctor Stone, that's precisely why the Parents First Alliance is interested in supporting Ben's bid for Congress." Randy stuck his nose into the discussion and his neck into the noose. Ali was quick to tighten the knot.

"Mr. Mason, you're either naive or uninformed."

Randy shoved his hands in his pockets, a sign he was offended. Good.

Ali continued. "As an attorney and Benjamin's close friend you should take time to review the court battles involving Mr. Boyd's organization. What the PFA wants is a hammer to come down on their side of court cases to earn big dollar donations. And in return I bet he's willing to pass some of that money on to the campaign you're planning to manage."

Both men blustered, insulted.

"Now, wait just a minute," Randy insisted.

"Who do you think you're speaking to, little lady?" Boyd demanded to know.

Ben was torn between pride for Ali and embarrassment for his involvement in the scene. Tomorrow he and Randy would go over their funding offers with a fine-toothed comb. Ben had to get some answers for himself, stop blindly accepting Randy's judgment.

"Gentlemen, please." Ben held his palms outward to silence any further discussion. "I'm afraid this impromptu meeting was not such a good idea after all. Dr. Stone has an appointment with Ethan and we need to speak beforehand."

He stepped to the left and motioned for Ali to see herself into the house. She moved inside without further comment. Simba, who followed close behind, paused to defend her mistress with a dark glance at Randy and soft growl for Boyd. Then the dog did something curious: she intentionally passed close enough to brush against Ben's pant leg.

Is she warning me or protecting me? Who knew with animals?

"I'm sorry about this," Ben began.

"That woman is the one who needs to be saying she's sorry," Boyd snapped.

Ben blinked several times, glanced from

Boyd to Randy and back again. "I was apologizing for not being able to meet with you. I don't know that Doctor Stone needs me or anybody else to apologize on her behalf."

"She does seem quite capable," Randy admitted.

Which is more than I can say for some people.

"Voilà!" Ali plunked four letters on the end of Ethan's last turn, then spelled aloud.

"B-L-I-N-D-N-E-S-S."

"Hey, you can't do that!" he insisted.

"Oh, yes I can," she corrected him. "Check the rules. I can add letters to the front or back of your words all day long."

He studied the guidelines printed in the top of the game box. She actually had no idea if what she'd done was legal or not, but Ethan cooperated as long as she kept him engaged in the game and that's all that mattered.

"And guess what else?" She smiled as Ethan looked up from his determined search to prove her wrong. "With my double-word bonus, I just turned your piddly score of eight into my whopping twenty-four!"

"A real mom would never take advantage of a kid like that," he muttered.

Her scalp prickled, signaling a teachable moment.

"Pleeeeease," Ali groaned. "First, I'm not a mom. And second, you can't expect me to believe your mother never got the better of you when you played games together."

"We didn't play that many games together." He kept his head down, perusing the list of rules.

"Then what did you two do for fun?"

"You're trying to distract me, so you can keep me from finding out you're cheating."

"Let me see that." Ali took hold of the box and pulled it from Ethan's grasp. She tossed it to the side. "Look, you can memorize the rules after I leave. If it turns out I was wrong, then we'll start off the next game with me fifty points in the hole."

Ethan's brows rose as he considered the offer. "Fair enough," he pronounced.

"Cool. So, tell me about hanging out with your mom."

"When I was little we spent a lot of time at the park or in our pool. And during soccer season she was always taking me to practice or watching my games."

"*Soccer?* Why not football, like your dad?"

Ethan grinned and for the first time Ali saw a pleasant memory gleam in his eyes.

"Mom used to say I started kicking and chasing a ball as soon as I could walk. She claimed I chose soccer just to get my dad's goat."

Ali fished for new letters. "Yep, sounds like typical father-son rivalry."

Ethan shook the head that had recently been washed and groomed, probably the pleasant surprise Benjamin had mentioned.

"No, it wasn't that way. I just didn't like seeing my dad and his friends getting pounded on the football field. I wasn't a sissy or anything like that." Ethan's eyes widened as he emphasized the point.

Ali took several mental notes. This was the first time she'd been able to get Ethan's mind off his obsessive subjects long enough to learn something about him firsthand. He cared how he was perceived, an encouraging indicator.

She glanced around his room. "I don't see any signs of you being a soccer fan. No posters or team colors."

"That was when I was a kid. I quit playing in middle school."

"How come?"

He waved away the subject. "Aw, it's lame."

"No, please tell me."

"Things changed." Ethan scrunched his face, ducked his chin and rubbed his left hand through the shaggy blond hair that fell over his forehead.

"I think that's when I caught Asperger's."

Ali wanted to smile at his choice of words, but humor now might spoil things. Instead, she nodded as if understanding.

"Ethan, tell me why you believe that."

The boy sat very still, examining his memory of the illness, maybe for the first time.

"Because I couldn't keep up. Soccer was too fast and too loud. People didn't stick to the game plan. I only cared about going to the library after that."

"Where you could study?"

He nodded. "And where it was quiet."

Another revelation. Middle school meant an adolescent surge of hormones, not an uncommon time for signs of mental illness to first appear or in the Asperger cases worsen. Instead of diving headfirst along with his peers into their teenage years, Ethan fashioned a world for himself that excluded everyone and everything except a subject he could master. And in his private world he'd found a hushed haven for the hearing that was becoming acute.

An idea was taking shape in Ali's mind.

"Ethan, when was the last time you visited the library?"

He ignored the question and took his turn instead. Carefully adding five tiles to the Scrabble board he spelled aloud, "A-Q-U-I-F-E-R. That's a rock formation that stores groundwater—"

Ali held a palm outward to block the beginning of a lecture. "I know what an aquifer is, professor."

"Just checking. Most people don't."

"How about answering my question now?"

Ethan's gaze locked on hers. The blue, blue eyes he inherited from his father gleamed.

"The last time we went to the library was the night my mother died."

Chapter Eleven

"I had no idea, Ethan. I'm sorry."

"Me, too."

Quiet settled over the room while Ali considered her next move, both in the game and in the boy's therapy.

"So, it's been several years then. How would you feel about a field trip to a library?"

He shook his head. "We went there a hundred times. They don't have anything that I can't find online now."

She relaxed into her plan and made a face as if his presumption had been absurd. "Not that little county facility whose leading-edge technology is a bookmobile. I'm talking about a big mack daddy library, the one over at Angelo State University."

Ethan drew his hand back from the work of sliding letters to the side in search of a *triple word score.*

She had his attention. *Thank you God!*

"Wouldn't their stuff be online, too?"

"Gimme a break," she scoffed, hoping he'd be curious enough to nibble the bait. "Aside from the bajillion volumes on the shelves, there are file drawers full of doctoral dissertations and brilliant theses papers that'll never see the light of day. And this is West Texas, baby. The gateway to the Permian Basin, the geologic capital of the Southwest! There's bound to be a lot on that subject."

He glanced sidelong at her comment, spotting the exaggeration for what it was.

"Okay, so there's no such claim to fame," Ali admitted. "But did you know some members of the faculty presented to the Geological Society of America where there were over ten thousand participants? Don't you think they have a little something over at Angelo State that might interest you?"

She'd read a tidbit on that subject in the local paper months ago and hoped her memory was somewhere close to accurate. It would be worth whatever forgiveness she had to beg later if it got Ethan out of the house now.

* * *

Ben rolled his shoulders and tilted his head side to side. He hadn't stretched sufficiently after his morning workout and the impromptu visit from Randy and Sanders Boyd had Ben's neck in a knot. Otherwise he'd be in his right mind and hearing Ali's comments correctly, though her odd behavior was certainly proof something good had happened.

If it was possible to skip down a flight of steps, she'd just done that very thing. Then Ali two-stepped across his living room floor to the accompaniment of David Letterman's theme song.

"I got Ethan to agree to go to the university library with me," she sung out of tune with the band.

"You did what?" Ben must have misunderstood. He'd offered everything under the sun just to get his boy to come downstairs. There was no way a simple invitation to the library had been the Holy Grail to get Ethan to leave the house!

"We made a date and we shook on it. As far as I'm concerned we're each going to live up to our part of the agreement."

It was late, after eleven o'clock, but her smile was alight with triumph. She'd been so tired when she'd arrived. This was not the same bedraggled Ali who'd gone upstairs over four hours ago.

"Where did you get this burst of energy?" Ben asked from the cushy comfort of his favorite chair.

As if she'd suddenly run out of steam, Ali stopped dancing about and plopped on the sofa, her head falling against a fat throw pillow. Simba started to follow suit but then remembered her manners. The dog paused and looked to him as if waiting for permission.

"Would you mind?" Ali asked, her lovely eyes pleading. "I gave her a bath this morning."

He was losing dominion over his territory, but there wasn't much left at this point anyway. More important, he was finding it difficult to deny Ali's requests, few though they were. If it put a glow in her otherwise tired face, it was worth his personal cost.

"Sure, why not." He gave in.

She stretched her legs, pressed close to the back of the sofa and patted the seat cushion in front of her body. With the grace of a gazelle, Simba leapt onto the couch, turned and then collapsed against her mistress, compliant as a stuffed toy. Ali spooned her pet, scratching and murmuring as the animal basked in the attention. Never having owned a dog, Ben had no earthly idea how it felt to share a physical bond with a four-legged creature.

Watching Ali and Simba commune through coos and kisses made Ben downright jealous of their unconditional companionship. It was foreign to him, completely missing in his life. Ali seemed to draw comfort and strength from caressing the sleek coat of her best friend.

Maybe someday he'd try to pet Simba.

When she was on a leash.

Asleep.

Heavily medicated.

He watched the two, envied their companionship. But mostly he longed to know the tender way Ali demonstrated her love through touch. What would it be like to have the woman softly stroke his shoulder, kiss his cheek, exhale a warm breath of contentment against his ear? Ben's memories of love weren't so deeply buried that he couldn't recall those sensations, didn't miss them every single day.

Wait a minute. That wasn't true at all. He hadn't been missing those things until very recently. From the afternoon Doctor Alison Stone had dropped out of the sky like a gift from heaven he'd begun to recognize a slow awakening in his heart as if from a deep, dreamless slumber. There was no denying it, he was feeling like a man again.

Ali straightened her knees, mindful to dangle the soles of her boots over the edge of the sofa. Her many bracelets clinked as she adjusted the hem of her calf-length denim skirt.

"Oh, it feels good to lie down. That second wind I got about an hour ago when things started to look up is amost gone." She stroked Simba's ears but fixed her gaze on Ben. Her eyes were wide, as if she'd discovered something surprising. "Ethan and I made real headway tonight."

Ben set the medical thriller he'd been reading to the side and slipped his glasses into his shirt pocket. "Tell me about it. Did you come up with a new strategy?"

She curved her lips in a lazy grin. "I'd love to take the credit, but it was more Forrest Gump than Freud. I asked a question about his mother and the conversation flowed from there. Before I knew it he was telling me all about her and their last day together."

Ben's enjoyable moment of seeing Ali as an appealing woman suddenly evaporated. Even though it shouldn't matter, the idea that she'd been talking with Ethan about his mother was unsettling. The loss of control intensified. It was possible Ali had learned things Ben didn't even know, and he was too embarrassed to ask what those things might be. He was a team player, always had been, but right now all six feet and four inches of him felt like the odd man out.

Lord, I have to speak up. Help me say the right thing.

"I'm grateful you've managed a breakthrough with Ethan, but now I'd appreciate it if you'd try to keep my late wife out of your conversations."

Ali's hands stilled. Simba turned accusing eyes on Ben as if sensing a mood change in her beloved mistress.

"Would you mind if I ask why you feel that way? We spoke about Ethan's mother before, and you never indicated that area might be off limits. In fact, isn't that what made you call me in the first place?"

Ben closed his eyes, not sure he even grasped it himself. Though he thought of Theresa every day, it was always in a pleasant way. By the merciful grace of God Ben's heart was healed, even ready to engage again as he was beginning to understand. But the sudden and tragic loss had reinforced the wall between himself and Ethan in a way that was too painful to have discussed behind his back.

"I guess I didn't even know it until just now." No other words came to mind, so he simply gave the same stupid shrug Ethan used when he wanted to avoid an uncomfortable answer.

"Well, that does tie my hands a bit, but our time together tonight may already have served the purpose God intended."

Ali was a true professional. If she was offended by Ben's irrational edict, she hid it well. She covered her mouth and yawned behind the palm of her hand.

"Goodness." She shook her head. "I guess the sugar rush has worn off from the two Snickers bars Ethan traded me for my malachite key ring."

Ben jumped up from where he'd been reclining. "I'm sorry for being such an inconsiderate host. Let me make you an espresso for the road." He headed toward the kitchen.

"A double shot in a to-go cup would be nice if you don't mind. Then I need to be on my way. I'm sinking fast."

"I'll pack you a sandwich, too." He called, his head poked inside the fridge. He pulled out a container of cold meatloaf and set it on the granite countertop beside the baguette of fresh sourdough bread. "Tomorrow's soon enough for you to tell me how you managed to get Ethan to agree to a field trip."

When there was no answer Ben presumed Ali either didn't hear him or she was in the powder room. He bustled about the kitchen, placed two halves of a thick sandwich in a zip lock bag, ground fresh espresso beans, added bottled water to the machine, then expertly drew two rich-smelling shots into his favorite travel mug. He smacked his hands together with satisfaction, picked up the lunch sack and coffee cup, then headed back into the living room.

"Ready when you are," he called.

But there was no sign of her. He moved closer until he could see over the cushioned back of the sofa. Ali lay on her right side, her head burrowed into the throw pillow. She snuggled Simba's back and draped her left arm protectively over the dog's belly, her nose buried in the silky neck. The woman was out like a light. Down for the count. Dead to the world. His father's silly expressions for deep sleep came to Ben's mind and they all applied.

He should wake her, put the cup of strong

coffee in her hand and send her on her way. Instead, he deposited his meager meal offering on the coffee table and bent closer. The tantalizing scent of honeysuckle shampoo hovered over silky hair Ben wanted desperately to touch. Her fair skin was lightly lined at the outer corners of her eyes, permanent signs of perpetual smiles.

She exhaled, a whisper of sound through softly puckered lips. Lips he would kiss if given the chance. Her thick auburn lashes rimmed lids that already twitched with REM sleep. Bent close as he was, it was impossible not to note the dark rings beneath Ali's closed eyes.

It was almost midnight. Her drive back into town was long and the road was too dark and desolate for a sleepy driver. Right or wrong, his decision was made.

Ben straightened, moved to the coat closet and pulled a spare quilt from the high shelf. He draped it carefully over the enchanting woman whose deep breathing never faltered. Simba lay motionless but her eyes followed his every move. Ben pressed his index finger to his lips as if she'd understand his signal, then he turned out the overhead light, leaving only the soft glow of a table lamp.

I really want to kiss Ali.

The idea was becoming comfortable to him as he looked back to where she lay, stunning yet vulnerable. If the dog were on the floor he might try to at least give his Sleeping Beauty a goodnight peck. It was best she was being guarded.

Ben smiled at the pair snuggled on his sofa and then crept to the master suite where he softly closed the door behind him.

A clock gonged somewhere. Ali didn't own a noisy timepiece. Her mouth was parched. Her tongue passed over her teeth, dry and nasty like a desert landfill. She squinted toward the windows on the far side of the room, not recognizing the expensive drapes or the view of the sun's glow that greeted the day. Simba grunted and stretched, pressing Ali back into sofa cushions.

Sofa cushions?

She sat up, tossed the unfamiliar quilt off her legs, bumped Simba to the floor and took in the surroundings.

Benjamin's house. And according to the mantle clock it was just after six in the morning. Still dark outside but not for much longer.

"Oh, good grief," Ali grumbled as she struggled to stand on feet that were swollen from being stuck in boots all night long. She didn't need a mirror to know her face was creased and puffy, her hair poking out in all directions.

"I'm too old for the walk of shame and I didn't even do anything to deserve it."

She grabbed her bag, motioned for Simba to follow and tiptoed to the front door praying the alarm hadn't been set. Either way, she'd make a run for it before anyone was the wiser. Boy howdy, would Erin Elise have a good laugh over this.

The silence of the early morning waited outside the door. She breathed in the glory of God's new day, wiped the sleep from her eyes while Simba did her business and then the two made quick work of leaving the exclusive neighborhood behind as they headed for town.

Three hours later Ali's cell phone hummed in her pocket. She reached beneath the desk, pressed the power button and motioned for her client to take a seat. She had a full day—calls could wait.

At two o'clock there was a tap on her office door before Josie poked her head inside.

"Sorry to bother you, Ali, but I noticed your calendar was clear for this hour and wanted to give you these phone messages. Your football player was really upset when I wouldn't put him through to you."

Ali thanked her young roommate and then glanced at the three while-you-were-out notes.

All from Benjamin. All marked *urgent*. Her bare arms tingled at the thought of being worthy of his attention, urgent or otherwise. Could these notes mean he was feeling the same restless need she'd been experiencing since they'd met?

She powered up her phone and it buzzed to life, full of messages from Benjamin. But instead of sounding excited he sounded anxious. She moved to the edge of her chair.

"What in the world is this all about?" She thought of Ethan and her heart quickened. Maybe he'd changed his mind. Or maybe he and his dad had words over their plans to visit the university library. After all, Benjamin had reacted oddly to Ethan's mother being at the center of last night's conversation. Anything could have happened this morning.

"I knew it," Ali admitted to Simba who snoozed on a doggie daybed in the corner. "I should have hung around instead of slinking off like I'd done something to be ashamed of. Better call and find out what's up."

Benjamin answered before the first ring was complete.

"Hello, this is Doctor Stone returning your calls," she wanted to sound professional.

"Ali, I've been trying to reach you for hours."

She clutched the cell phone tightly. Her empty stomach quivered. And not in the good way it had moments earlier.

Please God. Not again.

Don't let it be Ethan.

Chapter Twelve

"What's happened?" Ali held her breath, waited for whatever Benjamin had to say.

"Someone phoned in a tip to the local paper last night. This is such a slow news area that they actually took it seriously and planted a photographer down the street from my home. When you left around daylight the guy took shots of you at the front door and then again driving away. He got closeups of your face and license plates. There's no doubt it's you, Ali."

She shivered again, this time relieved. So, nothing was wrong with Ethan after all. *Thank you, Father.*

But to think some creep had actually hidden in the dark so he could watch and photograph her—what a rotten thing to do.

"But why? It's no secret that I'm working with Ethan. And plenty of people know he's refused to leave the house for the past few weeks. What can they possibly make of this and why would anybody care about me anyway?"

She heard Benjamin's sigh.

"This isn't about you, Ali. But it's about using you to embarrass me. And for that I'm terribly sorry."

"But who would do that?" As soon as the words were out she had a light bulb moment. "Oh, it's that Sanders Boyd jerk, isn't it?"

"I had the same thought. He knew you were there and he certainly left with a hornet under his hat. But there are plenty of other people who don't want me to run for Congress and they'd stoop to some pretty low stuff to keep me out of the race."

She glanced at the time, it was much later than she'd realized.

"I've been busy in my office all day. How did you find out about this? Is it already in the media?" Ali wondered if damage control was necessary. And what could she do, anyway? "Surely nobody will take this seriously."

His laughter was bitter in her ear.

"That's the most ridiculous part of all.

They'll know there's nothing to it. But not only will my opponents make something of it for their own gain, a few of my family members will, too."

"What makes you say that about your own family?"

"I got a call this morning from my second cousin. He's the editorial chief at the *Standard-Times*. Good old Gerald wanted to warn me they'll be running your photo on the front page of the evening edition and the headline will read 'Has Rescue Turned To Romance?' They'll follow up with a tabloid-style story about your involvement with Ethan and me since the incident in Big Bend."

Ali closed her eyes and groaned. If the Sunday Kids got wind of it they'd have a field day but mostly poking fun at their straight arrow of a counselor.

"He's your flesh and blood. Why won't he cut this off at the source?"

"Because it will sell papers and that's the bottom line in this economy. At least he gave me the opportunity to comment."

"And what did you tell him?"

"The truth! And as soon as he sells a few extra papers he'll probably print the facts and that'll ease his conscience. But by then the damage will be done."

She heard the umbrage in his voice. Felt the same. But his worries seemed more important than her own.

"Benjamin, the people who know you well won't take this seriously. And other than a bunch of grief from the guys on my rescue team I don't feel I have anything to fear, either."

But Ali's reconnection with her sister was so new and untested she couldn't make any assumptions about Erin's reaction. Maybe there was the possibility for more fallout than Ali knew.

"Hopefully, this will blow over in a day or two," she tried to comfort them both.

"Nobody would like to see this in a positive light more than me, but I have to be realistic. The Lamar name is both a blessing and a curse. Even though we have a legacy of service to the statc, thcrc's plcnty of opposition who would like to see our political dynasty die of unnatural causes."

"Surely what you stand for is more important than your last name."

"One would hope that's true. But then again, if *your* feelings about my positions and affiliations are an indicator, I'm a loser either way," he grumbled into the phone.

Ali held her breath, afraid any comment from her would be unwelcome. Would this incident make her persona non grata in the world of Benjamin and Ethan Lamar? The painful jolt of asking herself that question was a shock to her senses. She wasn't prepared to lose Ethan.

Or Benjamin.

"Ali, I was only teasing," his voice was soft. "That was my poor attempt to poke fun at myself before everybody else lines up to do it for me."

Relief swept her like a fan stirring a warm room. "I know you're concerned, but we've got to trust that God will work this out for our good."

"I hate to suggest this because I don't want to offend you, Ali. But I think it would be best if you didn't come back to the house again. At least not anytime soon."

"That's actually what I was going to discuss with you last night before I passed out on your couch. If I'd just gone on home it would have saved us this mess."

"All my fault. I made a decision and it backfired on me."

"I'm detecting a pattern in the area of you

making decisions for other people," she deadpanned.

"Ain't that the truth? My stock is dropping by the hour so I'd better stop offering up suggestions. Why don't you tell me what you had in mind?"

She leaned forward and scratched notes on the desk pad, then brought Google search up on her PC.

"Ethan agreed to visit the university library with me." She couldn't keep excitement from returning to her voice. "You should have seen his face when we got online and found out they have an exhibit hall dedicated to the geology of West Texas. His eyes lit up and I knew I'd found a magic bullet. I decided right then not to come back to your house so he won't get a chance to back out. But I need a few days to do some legwork first, get some special approvals."

"Do you want my help?" Benjamin offered, sincerity displacing his worry.

"You know somebody at the university who can give us exception clearance? I'd like to take Ethan on a day they're not open to the public or even after hours so he can get close to the exhibits, touch and feel to his heart's desire."

"Let me take a look at the school Web site

and check the list of department heads. There's bound to be a Lamar cousin in the ranks who can get you behind the velvet rope." He sounded pleased to have purpose, something to distract him from this fiasco.

"This must be one of those times when the name is a blessing, huh?"

"From your lips to God's ear. I'd better get on it right away before they have the chance to see tonight's paper."

"Benjamin, we'll get through this together."

"Thanks, sweet lady."

Ali flipped her phone closed. She typed her name and then his into the Internet search field and pressed the Enter key. There was no need to wait on the evening edition of the paper or the six o'clock news. The Congressional hopeful and the therapist for his autistic son were already a hot topic.

Her chin sagged and she shook her head. The woman in the photo looked like a troll who'd just crawled out from under a bridge. Her clothes were hopelessly rumpled. And that hair! Well, it was another story altogether. But Ali had to hand it to the photographer. The picture was crystal clear, and the subject was undoubtedly Doctor Alison Stone.

Yep, the guys at West Texas Rescue were going to have a field day with this! At that hour of the morning she'd looked more like a lump than the woman they called the Rock.

"Okay if I come in, boss?" Josie called.

"Sure, I could use a sympathetic ear. But aren't you supposed to be studying for an exam?"

"Awww, microbiology can wait a few more minutes."

Ali's roommate closed the door behind her and dropped onto the cozy patient's couch.

"Is this about you not comin' home last night?"

"Whoa, talk about cutting to the chase."

"Well, you're the one who taught me honesty is the best policy."

Ali winced. "I hate it when my own words bite me on the backside."

"Are you gonna give me the details or do I hafta wait and get them on *Entertainment Tonight?*"

"Oh, my gosh, Josie! What have you heard?" Ali's gasp of disbelief sent the young woman who'd once been among the ranks of the Sunday Kids into giggles.

"Oh, it's no big deal—just a little gossip in the cafeteria. Some people were makin' a mountain out of a fire ant hill but I straightened 'em out. Folks at this medical center should know by now that Doc Stone is a good egg."

Ali felt the warmth in her cheeks begin to rise again. How embarrassing to have the nursing student who'd literally pulled herself up out of the gutter be the person to rush to Ali's defense. But, by the same token, how amazing. God was constantly showing them how He used Satan's evil deeds for His own glory.

"So, are you gonna tell me what's going on with you and the football player or what? That guy's quite a catch, you know." Josie was totally enjoying Ali's discomfort.

"Will you stop! I'm not looking to *catch* anything. And, before you even ask, I am *not* dangling any bait, either. I've spent a lot of hours at the Lamar house, as you know, but mostly upstairs trying to get some traction with Ethan, which is about as hard to come by as a winning lottery ticket. But late last night, thanks to my sister suggesting a game of Scrabble, I had a breakthrough of sorts with the kid."

"Cool!"

"Very. But by the time I went downstairs to tell Benjamin about it I was dead on my feet, fell asleep on the sofa and he let me stay there overnight so I didn't fall asleep at the wheel. He meant well, and I left as soon as I woke up."

"Really?" Josie sounded disappointed. "That's all there is to it?"

"I know, pretty boring stuff, huh?"

"I was kinda hoping that boy's therapy wasn't the only *traction*, as you call it, in that house."

Ali ignored the innuendo. "Benjamin's definitely a better person than I originally gave him credit for being, but beyond that, the man's plate is full."

"If things were different, would you be interested?"

Josie just wouldn't let up. Ali leaned back in her chair to ponder the question. The thought had occurred to her more than once, but she'd dismissed it as single lady's daydreaming. But hearing her young friend say it out loud gave it credibility somehow. Not that it mattered, since Benjamin had been a perfect gentleman. He'd done nothing more than pay her one compliment, and that was probably out of pity since she was a mess by the time she made it to his house each evening.

"Well, would you?" Josie persisted. "You're always telling me to be open to new opportunities because a girl never knows what the Lord has planned."

"Yeah, well, right now I am praying He has a minor miracle planned. If I don't get Ethan away from the house and into a public place, I can't continue to see him."

"Or his famous daddy."

Ali nodded.

"Is that decision your doing?" Josie continued to press.

Ali hesitated before admitting, "Actually, it's Benjamin's, and I don't have much say about it."

Confessing her dependence on a man to another woman who was a victim of sexual abuse was like having a crowd of people witness an awkward fall and scraped, bloody knees.

It was mighty embarrassing.

And unbelievably painful.

Chapter Thirteen

Ben's day was not getting any better.

Soon after his conversation with Ali, Randy had called with the news that the story was already way past damage control. And to make matters worse, Laura Epps was now an official contender. From her seat on the board of the American Paint Horse Association she represented a growing source of financial power that couldn't be ignored.

"Buddy, it's declare now or call it off. With this Fort Worth woman putting her name on the ballot you've got to get in the game," Randy insisted, chomping at the bit for a decision. "This is national fodder, my friend. You're a football hero turned motivational speaker. Anybody who doesn't know you from the Cowboys' roster ought to recognize you from that infomercial you did with Tony Robbins. Did you really think this wouldn't go beyond the city limits of San Angelo?"

Ben couldn't remember being this conflicted since his senior year at UT when he'd been called up in the pro draft. Finishing his education had been the right thing to do because the NFL had waited. But there was little chance the U.S. Congress would be so patient. After the debacle of a meeting at his home last evening, Ben wasn't even sure he wanted his old friend calling major shots anymore. He really needed to do some big time praying and then counsel with somebody who wasn't invested in his decision. Someone who would help him weigh the facts without emotions clouding the picture.

Ali came to mind immediately. But he'd asked her to stay away, and for both their sakes they needed to stick with that plan.

"I guess expecting that photo to stay contained was pretty naive, huh?" Ben answered Randy's question.

"I'll say. And you've got to dump that Pollyanna thinking if you expect to survive in Washington. The opposition will eat you alive once they realize you're a card-carryin' Christian."

"Now just a cotton pickin' minute." Ben's hackles went up.

"Don't get bent out of shape, you know what I'm sayin'. Ben Lamar always tries to do the right thing, plays by the rules, gives his best and expects the same from everybody else. That's your reputation and it's an honorable one. But you can bet your last dollar some people will see your morals as a soft underbelly. And if you don't guard against that perception, you're going to get set up and knocked down more times than a stack of children's blocks."

"I don't much care for the way you're talking to me today," Ben warned.

"Well, that makes two of us because I don't care at all for the way you've been talkin' the past couple of weeks." Randy's voice reflected his exasperation. "This isn't something that just came up recently in casual conversation, you know."

Ben nodded, sitting alone at his desk. His friend was right. They'd been strategizing about this for ages. Randy was committed, ready to dive in over his head. But Ben was still reluctantly dog paddling in the shallow end.

"Yeah, I know," he admitted.

"Then fish or cut bait. Make up your mind,

Ben. I'd sure like to see you win that seat but if you're not up to the challenge, then admit it."

Ben bristled again. "Man, you're just pushing all my buttons today."

"Good!" Randy chided. "I'm done being patient. If you're not my candidate I'll go find another horse to back, if you get my drift." Even the hint of making Laura Epps his choice was going too far.

"Randy, we've been buddies for a lot of years. The last thing I want to do is lose our friendship over words. So, watch how you speak to me."

"You're right. That was out of line and I apologize." Randy's voice had lost its zeal. Ben wasn't sure that was a good thing. His friend fired a parting shot. "I'm going to back off and do a lot more thinking about my own business and not so much about yours. When you're ready to talk you know where to find me."

The line went quiet, leaving Ben feeling very much alone. Very much in need of the company of a certain redhead in noisy jewelry.

But he'd decided it was in everybody's best interest for her to stay away from the house. Well, if Ali couldn't come to him, he'd find a way to go to her.

* * *

Two days later, Saturday morning, no appointments. Ahhhhh…

Ali's sneaker was crooked on the edge of her kitchen counter as she stretched her hamstrings. It was a perfect day to get in a long run and some training for the upcoming competition. A knock rattled the front door of her town house.

"You gonna get that?" Josie called from her bedroom.

"Sure thing." Ali answered, knowing how the girl treasured having a bed to lounge in on the weekends after so many months of homelessness. "Who could that be?"

Simba hopped to her feet, moved to the door and pressed her long nose to the crack as if sniffing out the answer. Ali put her eye to the peephole. She encountered a fingerprint instead of the face of the visitor. Simba's lack of reaction implied there was nothing to fear. Still, opening a door without knowing who stood on the other side got women killed every day.

"The choice is yours, stranger. Reveal yourself or prepare to deal with Simba."

"It's only me!" Benjamin shouted. "Look out the window."

A silly grin curved her lips. Her heart surged

at the unexpected sound of his voice. She stepped to the glass panes above the sofa and slid back drapes still closed against the daytime sun. The sight of Benjamin on her front doorstep shouldn't have made her heart sing. But it did.

Oh, Lord, thank you! I needed this.

Since she'd spilled her beans to her roommate, Ali's mind had turned Josie's comments every which way but loose. Yes, there had been some momentum in the Lamar home apart from her work with Ethan. Her boldness caused Benjamin to re-examine his political bedfellows. He'd nearly quit flinching each time Simba came close. And even though he'd reacted badly to Ali and Ethan discussing his mother, Benjamin had mentioned his late wife enough times for Ali to suspect the sadness of the loss may have passed but some anger still lingered. Time and prayer would heal that wound, she was certain.

Benjamin waved cheerfully when he saw her part the drapes. He was the last person she'd expected at her door this morning, but if given the chance to make a wish list, this might very well have been in the number one spot.

"Simba, back." Ali was unabashedly excited.

Simba moved away from the entry, relaxed on her haunches. She waited patiently, lovingly, watching for a new command.

Ali turned the dead bolt and pulled the handle. Amazing eyes glinted from beneath a gray Dallas Cowboys cap emblazoned with a single star.

"Well, good morning Congressman," she chided.

He snatched the cap off and his gaze shifted downward.

"Do you have to keep calling me that? You say it like it's an insult."

"And that bothers you?"

Benjamin's head snapped up, his gaze pierced hers.

"Of course it bothers me. You're important to me, to my life, Ali. Having your respect matters a great deal."

The layers of this man were peeling back one by one. His positive nature wasn't a fake or a facade—he truly was a glass-half-full person. But each time she scratched a bit deeper she found him hurting a little more. They had a lot of things in common after all.

She touched his bare forearm below the short sleeve of his casual white shirt. His skin was warm beneath her cool fingertips. "Benjamin, I assure you that you have my respect."

"Thank you," his words were humble. "But not your vote, right?"

His teasing smile was back as he tugged the cap in place.

"That all depends on whether or not you're running. Have you made a decision yet?" She was relieved the serious moment had passed. More headway had been made.

If she could just say the same about Ethan.

"The only decision I made this morning was to get my kid out of the house." Benjamin turned and pointed toward the parking area. Two empty spots away from Ali's dirty Land Rover, a huge red convertible was backed in as if ready for a quick getaway. In the front passenger's seat was the back side of a familiar shaggy, blond head that wagged to and fro.

"Ethan!" Ali shouted as she hurried to the end of her private walkway. But the teen gave no indication of hearing. Benjamin followed behind, laughing at her efforts to get the boy's attention.

"He's wearing those little earbud things so he can tune out the traffic noises and listen to his iPod. I'm pretty sure his eyes are closed behind those gosh-awful sunglasses. Don't ask me where he dug up those checker boards."

"They're mine," she admitted. "He won them from me fair and square. How did you ever get him into the car? And where did that land yacht come from, anyway?"

They'd stopped at the end of walk, still a ways from where Ethan jived to his private concert, seemingly unaware they were even in the vicinity.

"One question at a time, please." Benjamin looked down at her, his eyes soft in their solemn stare. "Ethan misses you and your dog. He wanted to see both of you. I told him that was only gonna happen if he got in the car and let me bring him here."

"Why didn't you call? Five more minutes and you'd have missed us."

"I tried. When you didn't answer I took a chance you'd be someplace close by where we could spot the two of you."

Ali patted her pockets. No cell phone. She snapped her fingers. "I left it attached to my jeans when I put on these running clothes. It must be in the closet floor with the rest of my dirty laundry." Yuck, he didn't need that clue about her sloppy housekeeping when his place was always immaculate. She hurried to change the subject. "Well, I'm thrilled things worked out the way they did." She beamed at his success with Ethan.

"I believe your next question was more of a disparaging comment, but you won't get my goat on this subject." Benjamin's chest inflated with pride as he held his arms wide to present the red convertible. "I call this beauty the Scream Machine. She's a 1969 Cadillac DeVille, all original parts. My dad bought her the same day she rolled into the showroom at Randall Motors, so she's been in our family for over forty years. Dad left the Caddy to me with the provision that she never have an owner who's not a Lamar."

"It must be something special to have a family history to be so proud of."

Benjamin shrugged, made light of his pedigree. "Oh, every parent thinks their child hung the moon and every child believes their parent is a superhero. Even if the sentiment only lasts a few minutes, I think it's pretty standard."

"Not necessarily," Ali muttered.

"Sorry, I forget you work with kids whose experience has been anything but that."

"And speaking of kids, let me get Simba and we'll come say hello to Ethan."

"I see you're dressed to go for a run, but how about going for a ride with us instead?"

She gave him a hard look. "Do you think that's wise after the media storm of the past few days?"

"Here's how I've come to look at it." The lines of his face relaxed as if peace rushed in where stress had been camped for ages. "You sleeping on our couch is pretty small stuff when you consider how many married Congressmen have been forced out of office over misbehaving with their college interns. If a budding romance between a widower and a single woman is the worst they can make of us, then I'd say we can survive it."

A budding romance? So, she wasn't imagining it!

"Come on, go with us," he cajoled. "A stop at the Marble Slab for a banana split with extra pecans was another condition of getting Ethan out of the house."

"I think I should be offended by being the same temptation as fruit and nuts, but I'll let it pass because the offer is just too good to resist." She looked toward the open door knowing Simba would still be waiting patiently, her belly pressed to the cool tile. "My roommate's inside. I need to let her know I'm leaving for a while so she can keep an eye on Simba. You have to promise to have me back in an hour. The Rescue Round Up is next weekend and we're not ready."

"Rescue Round Up?"

"I'll tell you over the most expensive sundae Marble Slab sells." She turned about face and headed for the door. A strong hand on her shoulder stopped Ali in her tracks and sent her pulse info a flutter fest.

"Thanks, Ali," Benjamin said softly. His gaze was as warm as his hand. "I figured something out over the past couple of days."

She held her breath, silently praying that the man standing before her would be the one she'd waited for all her life. A gentleman whose very presence was enough to help her forget the past. To give her hope for a future.

"Ali, Ethan may have missed you, but I've been downright lonely without your company. I know we disagree on some important things, but can we focus on the areas where we think alike and see where it leads?"

"Sure." She smiled, not knowing how else to answer. "I'll meet you at the car in two minutes." She turned toward her door.

So, that was it. Since their conversation

about his wife Benjamin had discovered he was lonely.

From her years of foster care and then being completely on her own as a student, Ali certainly knew the power and depths of that emotion.

Well, Benjamin hadn't exactly made a declaration of love, but it was a start they could build on.

Wasn't it?

Chapter Fourteen

"So, why did you spend so many nights hanging out at the house and then just stop showing up? What kind of flaky doctor does that to a kid?"

"Ethan! Where are you manners?"

"It's okay." Ali assured Benjamin she hadn't taken offense. "We agreed the first night to shoot straight so he's entitled to his opinions." She turned her attention on Ethan. "I'm entitled to mine, too. And you know what I think? I think you are selectively disabled."

Ethan paused momentarily from the business of shoveling ice cream into his face as if someone might take the rest away at any moment. Ali was continually amazed by the eating habits of teenage boys. Even Simba showed better sense, taking her time over the dinner bowl.

"What does selectively disabled mean?" he mumbled with his mouth full.

"It means you have control over when you panic and when you remain calm. That choice is always within your ability. *You* have to decide when and how to exercise the control, just as you are today."

"So, you're saying I've been faking it?"

"No, you're definitely a mental case." Ali paused, waited for the smirk she knew the inappropriate comment would get from Ethan. "What I'm saying is you're lazy. Kiddo, when you're motivated your abilities are far beyond what you give yourself credit for. And one day soon I'm going to prove that to you."

She took another luscious spoonful of sweet cream and cookie dough, then looked to Benjamin for his reaction. For the most part he'd steered clear of her discussions with Ethan, not judging or interfering. Today he seemed to be doing the same. If it bothered Benjamin for Ali to criticize or issue challenges, he didn't let it show.

"So, when are you two going to have this outing at the university library?" Benjamin asked.

Ethan stopped scraping his plastic spoon

around the edges of his container. "Yeah, when? I really need to know."

Asperger's made the boy rigid about his schedule, so Ali understood his need for a timeline. But even with a plan he could still get overanxious and refuse to cooperate. Because today had been so successful, she felt the element of spontaneity might be more effective than days of planning and hours of worry over the timing.

"Patience is a virtue you know so little about, Ethan. But I'm working out the details," she said softly, knowing it was not the answer he wanted.

"You promised," Ethan whined. He pushed his bottom lip out, once again reverting into his childish other-self.

She glanced at Benjamin, noted the tense set of his jaw, the building aggravation. It had to be difficult for such a driven and successful father to watch his only son morph from snotty teen to insecure child in the blink of an eye. Neither was attractive and both were disappointing. She prayed they would make further strides together. But Ethan was who he was and only God's hand could permanently change that circumstance. Benjamin may have to be the one to change instead.

She risked touching Ethan's arm in an effort to reassure him. "Yes, I promised and I keep my promises. We're going to have a fabulous time, and we could go right now if we wanted to be around a bunch of other people. But if you'll hold your horses a couple more days you'll get a closer look at everything. Okay?"

Eyes downcast, Ethan nodded as he slipped his hands beneath the table outside of her reach.

Benjamin shrugged and pursed his lips, an unspoken *What did you expect?*

Ali checked her watch. "Guys, the ride in the Scream Machine was awesome and the sundae was fabulous. I will cherish it for weeks to come." She patted the side of her hip knowing her comment wasn't entirely a joke. But the rest of her day would require a lot of energy. Maybe she'd burn some of the calories before they took up permanent residence on her thighs.

"We'll head back just as soon as you tell us about this Rescue Round Up you mentioned before."

"Oh, right." She needed to bring Ethan back into the conversation so he wouldn't sulk all afternoon and spoil the day with his dad. "Hey, you remember Harry and Sid don't you? They were the crew who lifted us out of Big Bend."

The boy grunted, sufficient encouragement to continue.

"Well, every year we get together with other rescue units to compete for team and individual honors. It's not anything official, just fun and braggin' rights, but you know how much that means to a Texan.

"Anyway, I participate with the guys from West Texas Rescue in the obstacle relay. I climb and rappel individually and then Simba competes against other working dogs in physical strength and commands." Ali turned to Benjamin who was listening intently enough to make up for Ethan's fixation on his empty cup. "That's a day when you can truly appreciate how smart she is. It might even make you want to pet her."

Benjamin shuddered, raising his shoulders to his ears and shivering as if something had just crawled up his spine. Ali laughed at his silly antics.

"Could I go?"

Ali and Benjamin swiveled their heads in Ethan's direction. "What?" they chorused.

"I want to watch."

"Sounds doable to me," Benjamin agreed as he turned to Ali. "Could we come?"

"It really isn't a fancy to-do, guys. I wouldn't want you to be disappointed when you show up at the park and it's just a make-shift obstacle course with a bunch of dare-devils eggin' each other on."

"How about this—we'll come cheer for you and after you and Simba win I'll take us all out for a celebration dinner?"

"Wow, that's a nice offer. What are you willing to do, Ethan?"

He jumped to attention. "What's this got to do with me? I just wanna watch."

"If we have to sing for our supper, you do, too. How about this? After the competition is over some of our family members get to harness up and climb the wall or put on knee pads and experience parts of the obstacle course. As long as you're willing to do one or the other you can come."

He slumped in the chair, silent.

Ben watched his son, almost certain he would refuse the challenge. But there was something about Ali that made Ethan want to please her, be close to her. Ben understood— he felt the same. Using her as bait to get Ethan out of the house today was pretty low. But it had worked! And now what had initially seemed disrespectful felt more like a stroke of genius. It gave Ben an open-ended excuse to be with Ali even if it was initially for his son's benefit. This bond between her and Ethan was just what Ben was praying for, so he'd grabbed the opportunity like a cornerback grabs an interception.

"Come on, buddy. That's fair and it sounds like a lot of fun. What do you say?" Ben encouraged Ethan, hoping he'd go along.

"It's not fair at all. Ali has to work hard and I have to try something scary. All you have to do is pay the bill and that's no big deal for you."

His son was right. "Okay, you name it. What do you want me to do to make it even?"

Ethan looked at Ali. The two gazes locked and the small nod that passed between them would have been missed by most people. For a split-second Ben felt a pang of jealousy. Someone had been successful where he'd failed. Just as Ethan and Ali had snickered over her "mental case" wisecrack before, the two had broken the nonverbal sound barrier right before Ben's eyes. The stinging moment of envy came and went like a puff of smoke in a gust of wind. Insignificant. All that mattered was moving Ethan forward. Giving back his life. Restoring their future and making Ali a part of it.

Whatever his son chose for Ben's part of the plan, it would be worth it.

"I know exactly what price you should pay." Ethan rubbed his hands together, enjoying the thought of what he had in mind. "Why don't you guess?"

"Okay, let me see," Ben pretended to think hard. "A new high-def television?"

Ethan shook his head. "Nope. Guess again."

"Umm, how about a driving lesson in the Scream Machine?"

"Nice, but keep guessing," Ethan insisted.

Ben glanced at the wall clock. "Ali has to get back to her house, so why don't you end the suspense?"

Mischief spread across Ethan's face in a way Ben hadn't seen in years. The triumphant look in his son's eyes was priceless.

Thank you for this moment, Lord!

"If I climb higher than ten feet you have to sit with your arm around Simba for five minutes," Ethan announced.

Ben's stomach lurched. He took a sip of water to force down the ice cream that threatened to surge up into his throat. His face filled with heat and prickles of sweat broke out beneath his cap.

He was afraid of that animal. Ethan knew it. Ali knew it. And when the time came the dog would certainly know it.

Ben couldn't refuse. Wouldn't refuse.

Ali laughed, a comforting sound even if it was at his expense.

"Smooth move, kiddo!" She praised Ethan, then turned to Ben. "So, what do you say? Are you gonna run with the big dogs or sit on the porch?"

"Good one, Ali," Ethan caught the obvious pun.

"I thought so." She beamed.

Ben stalled his response with a question. "Is there any chance this was a setup?"

"What difference does it make, Dad?"

"Yeah, Benjamin. You're the one who threw down the gauntlet. Now, what's it gonna be?"

Ben willed his gut to stop the nervous churning it had experienced at the nearness of a dog for as long as he could remember. To his parents' recollection, there had been no trigger event to cause the trauma. He'd tried hypnosis once to exorcise the embarrassing reaction.

When that failed he reconciled to keeping a barrier between himself and canine creatures. And it had worked until Ali had become part of his life.

"Come on, Dad. Don't be a chicken."

"How can I possibly refuse such heartfelt encouragement from my son?"

"So, you're in?" The incredulous note in Ethan's voice was second only to the delight in his eyes.

"Yes, count me in."

The cheer that went up from their small table drew more stares than usual. Ben glanced around and smiled apologetically. His eyes stopped on a familiar face. He raised his hand in a half-hearted wave, then groaned quietly when his cousin left the waiting line for the popular ice cream parlor and headed their way. There was no time to whisper a warning.

"Well, if it isn't the family celebrity." The tone was light but not enough to cover what was intended as a biting comment.

"Hello, Gerald." Remembering the good manners his mama had taught him, Ben stood and extended his hand. "Ali, this is my cousin, Gerald Lamar. He's the editorial chief at the

Standard-Times. Gerald, this is Doctor Alison Stone. Of course, you know Ethan."

Gerald ignored Ethan and focused on Ali.

"I'd recognize Doctor Stone anywhere and I must say the pictures I've seen didn't do her justice."

"As much as I'd like to take that as a compliment I know the photos you're referring to and even a brown paper bag over my head would have been an improvement."

Her lips were pressed together as if she had more to say. She didn't stand or offer her hand.

Good for you, Ali.

"I doubt you're interested in an accurate quote, but you may repeat me as saying your publication showed incredibly poor taste in choosing a few pieces of silver over the facts."

Gerald laughed. "Ah, she's a spunky one, Ben. No wonder you're out having ice cream with her when you should be hosting a political fundraiser. Or are you still on the fence over whether or not to run?"

"When I've made a decision you and the rest of our family will hear it first and from me."

"I hope you'll give the *Standard-Times* an exclusive. You know we'd strongly consider endorsing you."

"Again, we'll have that discussion when it's appropriate."

Gerald glanced toward the parking lot, then engaged Ben in a stare down.

"It's a nice day to be cruising in your daddy's big Cadillac. But you know Laura Epps hit the ground running as soon as she announced her campaign. According to our poll she's already ahead of you and the other wannabes because she's proved she's in it to win it. The longer you hold out, the more people are gonna think you've lost your edge. But I know you'll make the right decision for Ben Lamar. You always do," he sneered. "If you can't stand the heat, stay out of the kitchen."

With his parting shot fired, Gerald nodded and left their table.

"He's a jerk." For once Ethan's bluntness was apropos. "Why did you let him speak to you that way? You shoulda punched him."

"Politics can be a mean business sometimes, son. And I let Gerald say those things because he's right. I've been on the fence too long."

Fish or cut bait.

Run with the big dogs or stay on the porch.

If you can't stand the heat, get out of the kitchen.

Ethan was sitting in a public place showing just the improvement Ben had been praying for. Now, his cousin's words were like the two-minute warning.

It was time Ben got his head and his heart in the game. This was sudden death with no instant replay.

Chapter Fifteen

Sunday was Ben's favorite day of the week, and it had nothing to do with football. Though he'd enjoyed the previous day's excitement with Ethan and Ali, Ben treasured the Sunday morning hours as he joined in praise songs that reverberated from his satellite radio. Then he worshiped at the church where he'd come to faith and been baptized as a boy, and finally ended the morning with a late brunch at the country club. With Mrs. Alvarez back from her vacation and at the house with Ethan, Ben was free to resume his weekend routine.

Waiting at his favorite table he glanced around at some of San Angelo's finest citizens. Well-heeled oil and cattlemen sat tall, proud of their expensively dressed wives. Ben grinned as he remembered scenes from the eighties television series set in Dallas where J.R. and Bobby had entertained lavishly at the Baron's Club. This room might be absent all the public drama, but the West Texas gentry seated nearby were every bit as proud of their heritage as the Ewing brothers.

A second and closer look failed to reveal even one natural redhead with a long braid and dangly silver earrings. It jolted Ben to the toes of his boots to realize he was no longer comparing the other women to Theresa.

The beauty on his mind these days was Alison Stone.

He grew warm sitting in the sunny window and signaled a nearby waiter to slant the blind. But even positioned in the shade the troublesome heat did not abate. And Ben knew why. The temperature increase was *internal*. The sensation had been happening for days and he no longer made the effort to deny the source of his discomfort.

He was falling in love with Ali.

She was under his skin and she'd tunneled right to his heart. She was amazing, talented, open and honest. Ethan was smitten by her approach to him and to life and Ben was admitting right here and right now, his future was moving in an unexpected direction and he seemed powerless to stop it.

If Ali weren't so adamant about her Sunday private time he'd have invited her to join him. Her down-to-earth approach to everything would help in today's dealings with Randy and the park conservation group Ben would be meeting in the afternoon.

"They said you'd be at your usual table." Randy's greeting was casual, as though their recent differences hadn't occurred. "You're gonna have to be a little less predictable when you get to Washington."

"What would you suggest I do differently?" Ben stood to give his friend a handshake and slap on the shoulder, then waited to see what pearls of political wisdom Randy would toss out today.

"Well, for starters, sit with your back to the wall so those liberals from the left coast can't sneak up behind you." He chuckled, only half joking.

"I'll take that under advisement." Ben picked up the menu, though he knew it by heart. He needed to avert his eyes for a moment while he considered the dark feeling that settled over him as Randy took a seat to the right. Was it switching gears from a loving revelation about Ali to the matter of his campaign that had Ben's spirit confused?

"Just a Cobb salad and ice tea for me," Randy told the waiter.

Ben ordered Eggs Benedict with freshly squeezed orange juice. His usual. He folded his hands and leaned on the table.

"Okay, tell me about these new folks you want me to meet. Where did you find them?"

"I'll be blunt, Ben. After that mess at your house between Doctor Stone and Sanders Boyd and then the way Boyd retaliated, I thought it best to move toward a less controversial subject. City park conservation and growth should be safe ground to get the campaign launched."

Ben held his palm outward. "Back up a minute. Are you telling me you know for sure Boyd is responsible for that photo in the media and all the junk Ali and I have put up with ever since?"

Randy leaned against his chair, taken aback by Ben's question.

"Well, I don't know for *certain*. I mean, he didn't call and brag to me or anything like that. But it's pretty obvious, isn't it?"

"I followed the same logic. I just feel badly about silently accusing the guy when I have no proof."

Randy shook his head. "I really don't get you, Lamar. We've known each other, what? Twenty-five years? And you never say a negative thing about another person, even when they deserve it. They won't know what to think of you on Capitol Hill."

"I hope they'll think I'm a Christian man who's committed to walking the walk."

"Okay, whatever." Randy reached into a sleek, black crocodile attaché case, pulled out several pages of handwritten notes and began coaching for the afternoon meeting.

Several hours later, Ben stood in the spreading shade of a majestic Chinquapin oak. He and a small group representing the Lend a Hand Foundation met at Halfway Landing, an antiquated city park in desperate need of rehabilitation. With newer recreational areas to choose from, this site was in serious decline and overgrowth. Sadly, the neglect not only affected a historic area where brave, western-bound settlers were buried, it also dragged down the property value of the homes of the nearby senior citizens who couldn't afford the move to more upscale, desirable neighborhoods.

Ben felt an instant connection with this project. Here was an area where he could literally roll up his sleeves and get involved. It might even be something he and Ethan could do together.

"So, now that you've seen the place you can probably understand why we were so excited when Mr. Mason contacted us. Having you announce your candidacy from this site will give our foundation some positive media attention." Mary Barker, the self-proclaimed ringleader of the group grinned and elbowed Ben. "A little something you and Doctor Stone could use, right?" she murmured conspiratorially.

As much as he'd thought the rumors about his private life would be water off a duck's back in a day or two, he'd been wrong. He was accustomed to being in the spotlight, took it in stride. But the insinuations about Ali had gone on too long.

"Mrs. Barker, that situation was entirely innocent, I assure you. If I had anything to be ashamed of I wouldn't be asking you fine folks to support me."

She ducked her head, probably wishing

she'd left the sensitive subject alone. When her eyes met his again they glistened with apology.

"I'm sorry for such forward teasing, sir. You're known to be a Christian man and I shoulda been more respectful. But I say it's always good to acknowledge the elephant in the room and then leave the door open so he can leave when he's ready." She shoved her hand outward and Ben grasped it, glad for the offer of friendship. "We're happy to have you on board with us, Mr. Lamar."

"Please, call me Ben." He glanced toward the cleared area in need of mowing, benches and tables that required repair and the surrounding woods overgrown with patches of briars and scrub brush. "Would you mind if I take a look around by myself? I'd like to step off the boundaries and see just how much reclamation work there is to be done. When I hold the press conference I want to be able to speak to this particular project from personal experience."

"Oh, please do. We need hands-on volunteers, folks who aren't afraid of muscle aches or grass stains. You'll be a perfect spokesperson." Her broad smile twisted into a frown of concern. "Only, take care about the south border of the property. The area along that fence line is always filthy with vagrant trash. When the sheriff has time to donate an afternoon we'll get it cleaned up. But everybody's afraid to go out there without a police escort. There's no tellin' what dangerous no-accounts hang out in those woods."

"I'll be careful," he promised, not believing there could be that much to worry about. So, a few transients left their burger sacks behind. How bad could it be?

Ben agreed to contact Mary that evening with a press conference date as soon as he spoke with Randy. The Lend a Hand volunteers headed home for Sunday supper and Ben changed into his hiking boots for a closer look at the park and cemetery.

By the time the fence ran out and made a ninety-degree turn to mark the southern border of the property, Ben was sweaty from the oppressive afternoon heat and itchy from mosquito bites that swelled up like goose eggs. But other than the buzzing of hungry flies the wood was mostly quiet.

What appeared to be a cluster of moss-covered stumps in the distance turned out to be a dozen or more crude grave markers. Ben dropped to one knee, gave thanks for the blessings in his life and prayed for the unknown souls of those long ago laid to rest beneath his feet.

"This isn't right. These people were courageous and they deserve respect, not an anonymous hiding place."

He imagined what the cemetery must have looked like almost two hundred years ago, chosen for its peaceful silence interrupted occasionally by chirping or croaking. It would take equipment and work to restore the setting, but it was doable and so worth the effort.

Voices in the distance brought Ben to his feet. He should turn back. He recalled the warning about "dangerous no-accounts" but his nerves were undisturbed by fear. He turned his hearing to the sounds and listened for anything audible. Now and again there was laughter, young male and female voices.

Kids?

He had to find out.

The thick cushion of brush absorbed his steps, keeping his approach quiet as he moved toward the sounds. A flash of color sent him ducking behind the thick trunk of an evergreen. He peered around the knobby bark feeling like a coward but figuring safe was better than sorry.

A woman's voice floated above the others,

sending a series of shivers down his spine like aftershocks following an earthquake.

Pop-ping! Pop-ping! Pop-ping! The quiet of the wood shattered with the tinny noise of pellets bouncing off a metal target.

The woman laughed and called out, "Y'all are gonna get us thrown in jail!"

The husky voice was unmistakable.

Ali.

Chapter Sixteen

Ali grimaced at the scabbed-over skull and crossbones on the backside of the young man's shaved head as he moved to set ancient soda cans back up on the fence posts. Lenny was the unofficial leader of her present crop of Sunday Kids. Abused and homeless, they kept Ali cognizant of the life she'd managed to escape and she gave them guidance and hope for the future. She was definitely on the winning end of their arrangement, grateful they trusted her enough to show up at this appointed place each week.

"Aww, jail ain't so bad, Doc," Lenny called across his shoulder. "I'd choose it over my old man's trailer in a hot minute. At least down at county you get a semi-private room and three squares a day."

How sad that at nineteen Lenny should be so knowledgeable about the correctional system. Sadder still that lockup was safer than being with his family.

But Ali understood.

"Lenny, I bet that new tat hurt." Carla scowled, her face crinkling like the wad of pink chewing gum she'd just stuck to the fallen tree where Ali was perched.

"You should know," Deena accused. "You got more ink than Tommy Lee."

Carla held both arms outstretched, admiring the full-sleeve tribal symbols she'd probably gone hungry to afford.

"Bug off, Deena Beana." Lenny teased both girls who were more like little sisters to him than the streetwise kids they'd been forced to become. "When are you gonna grow some courage and do more than poke holes in your face?" He ambled back from the tower of cans and prepared to reload his ancient pellet gun for Carla's turn.

"If I get accepted into nursing school someday like Josie did, I can take the ring out of my eyebrows and lips. What are you gonna do—wear a stocking cap the rest of your life to cover your *artwork?*"

"Ever heard of growing hair?" Carla asked as she reached for the weak excuse for a target practice pistol.

"Not that a full head of hair is of any interest to me." She chuckled, then patted her one hot pink strand that swooped the top of her head, á la Donald Trump.

All four broke into a fit of silly laughter as if they hadn't a care in the world.

"Okay, okay, that's enough." Ali dug into the backpack for provisions. She tossed sandwiches, candy bars and juice boxes around the makeshift camp. The teens pretended disinterest before tearing into the food. Looking down into Simba's eyes Ali feared these kids might never learn to trust as simply as her pet did.

Father, bless this meal to the nourishment of their brutalized bodies and give me words of wisdom and compassion to make a difference in their lives.

The silent prayer she sent up would have to be enough. They'd scurry like wood rats if she dared to reach out with anything more.

During another round of snacks the three forgot Ali was from the outside and talked about their dreams. Yes, even kids on the street want better. Josie was a success story Ali hoped to replicate many times over. No, she couldn't bring every Sunday Kid into her home, but Josie had taken bold steps on her own toward education. With a little short-term support and encouragement, she was on her way to a secure future.

A tiny red light winked from the BlackBerry clipped to Ali's belt. A quick peek at the screen said it was the message she'd hoped for. Deena noticed the distraction.

"Hey, I thought you said you were gonna get rid of that thing."

Ali smiled at the idea. "That was just wishful thinking on a day when I was tired. Y'all know I'm on call twenty-four seven. If I got rid of this high-tech gadget, the rescue dispatcher couldn't reach me and neither could you if you ever wanted to try." She stood, handed over the camo backpack she'd found at a thrift store for Lenny.

"Gotta go?" There was disappointment in his voice, a far cry from the first time she'd shown up at their spot.

"Yep. Duty calls."

"But this is our Sunday time and tomorrow's a holiday. Why don't you tell them to leave you alone?"

"Maybe I don't want to be left alone." And

maybe one day, with God's help her Sunday Kids wouldn't either.

Ali silenced the *60 Minutes* news show with the mute button, leaned against the soft leather of her modular sofa and toed off her sneakers to plop bare heels on the ottoman.

She punched Benjamin's private number into her cell and waited for his answer. Even after leaving two messages on the home phone he hadn't returned her calls. If he didn't pick up this time she'd get back into the Land Rover and make the drive out to his place to reassure herself nothing was wrong and to surprise Ethan with her news in person.

"Ben Lamar here," his voice was brusque. Was she intruding?

"Hey, it's Ali."

"Are you okay?" he snapped, sounding more like Ethan than Benjamin.

"Yes, of course. Why would you ask that?"

"How about because you've made it clear your Sundays are off limits to me and Ethan and you've never called me on this line before."

"Oooookay, well, I have some news that can't wait and there was no answer on your house phone."

"I'm cleaning the pool on the odd chance Ethan might want to use it tomorrow while we're out back."

It sounded like Ben was expecting company for Memorial Day. Could he have a date? *Well, of course he could, Einstein! He's only the most eligible bachelor in the Lone Star State.*

Her spirits plunged at the thought.

"Oh, I'm sorry to interrupt."

"You're not interrupting anything that can't wait. Tell me what's so important." He reminded her of the reason for the call.

"I know tomorrow's a holiday and you seem to have plans, but could you drop Ethan off at the university in the morning? I'd come get him myself but I don't want to stir up any new trouble for either of us."

"You got the clearance you needed?" He seemed pleased, less tense.

"Yep, the message came through a little while ago. The security guard has instructions to let us into the geologic exhibit and give us free access. It's not like we can do a lot of damage to hunks of rock anyway, but I hear the library houses some rare fossils, priceless kinda stuff. By the way, did you know Texas has a state dinosaur that lived during the early Cretaceous period?"

"No, but I'm positive Ethan does. I'll be sure to remind him to look and not touch."

"So you'll bring him?"

"Of course," Benjamin agreed.

Ali wanted to clap her hands like an excited kid.

"If you can get him out of the house early then it won't interfere with the rest of your day. I'll drive him home myself if necessary."

Benjamin didn't respond. It was quiet on his end for so long Ali began to think he'd gone back to sweeping the pool.

"Benjamin? What do you think?"

"I think it sounds like I'm not invited."

Ali's breath caught, her heartbeat quickened. "I thought you just said you had plans."

"I have plans to dig up an old flower bed so I can plant an herb garden and then eventually grill some burgers. I gave our housekeeper the day off so she could hit the holiday sales. Mrs. Alvarez always loads up on school clothes and ships them across the border to her nieces and nephews in Juarez. I offer to cover the cooking on holidays, since I never go anyplace anyway."

"Is that a hint?"

"Yes," he admitted. The man was appealing even when he pouted.

"Benjamin, anytime you want to participate in our therapy outings you're welcome to join us. *You* are the one who got Ethan into that car the other day so you produced the breakthrough. I have neither reason nor desire to keep anything from you." That *sounded* altruistic anyway. The truth was she wanted Benjamin along but didn't know how to ask without sounding needy. "As far as I'm concerned, the more you share in Ethan's progress, the better. You're a great influence and an incredible role model."

"Thanks for such kind words." He was quiet again for a few moments. "You *said* you'd begun to respect me, but a person can never be sure."

She considered his words. There was hope in the statement but sadness in the delivery. What had happened since she'd seen him the day before?

"Benjamin, is there something you need to tell me?"

"As a matter of fact, I do have some news to share. I've finally made the decision to run for the open Congressional seat. I'll be announcing my candidacy as soon as Randy can arrange the details of the press conference."

Ali stiffened, raised her spine away from the

comfy sofa. Would Benjamin still accept support from the Parents First Alliance? Even if he didn't the political action committees of Texas would line up at the door to fund the election of Benjamin Lamar in exchange for favorable votes down the road. It was the way politics operated in America, like it or not. She'd hoped against hope that he'd decide not to run.

Her insides clenched and churned at the thought of Benjamin shifting his full attention away from the welfare of his son. Instead he'd be giving his time to the writing and passing of laws, important things, but not compared to matters of the heart.

Specifically her heart.

I'm in love with Benjamin. She felt it in her core, had known it for days but hadn't fully made the admission. Until now.

That's what this is really all about. Ali selfishly feared for her own needs, more than she cared about Ethan's welfare or Benjamin's dreams. For the first time in her life, she'd begun to care for a man. And now she was afraid for herself. But it was a fear that made her want to move closer, not back away safely behind the walls she found so comforting and therapeutic. So impenetrable.

Still, she had to know which way Benjamin was headed in his political thinking.

"Will Sanders Boyd be at your side when you make the announcement?" She went fishing for information.

"That's unlikely, but you can never tell who might turn up to support us in the coming months. You know I care about family rights and I won't burn any bridges that I may need to cross in the future."

It was a straight answer even if it wasn't the one she wanted. Benjamin deserved high marks for honesty and political speak.

"I guess I should give you my congratulations."

"I'd prefer your vote."

She shook her head. It always came back to that.

"Nothing's changed. How I cast my ballot will depend on the issues you stand for and the political bedfellows who turn out to be part of your camp."

"That's fair enough. Would you consider coming to the rally when I announce my intention to run?"

She closed her eyes and dropped her chin. She didn't want to be one of many in a crowd around the candidate and she couldn't afford to be singled out. Benjamin was moving forward with his plans. Ali had to do the same and that meant protecting her practice. She didn't need the hassle of defending against rumors any more than he did.

"I don't think that would be wise, but how about if I offer to hang out with Ethan that day? He's not up to a noisy crowd or being the center of attention yet. So, just give me some notice and I'll plan to spend the day with him when your press conference takes place."

"That probably makes more sense. But could you at least watch it on television? It would mean a lot to know you're out there somewhere."

"Sure. Where are you going to hold the rally?"

"There's some very old public acreage on the edge of town. It was one of the first official parks in the county and it's fallen on hard times. I'm going to partner with the Lend a Hand Foundation to get it cleaned up and re-dedicated to the city network."

Ali's nerves sizzled with tension. "Are you talking about Halfway Landing?"

"That's the place," Benjamin confirmed. "So much good can be done there for the local community once we get it restored. But first the sheriff needs to take care of the undesirables squatting out there making a mess of city property."

The undesirables. He means my Sunday Kids—people like Deena, Carla and Lenny. People like Josie.

And me.

Chapter Seventeen

Ben woke early Monday morning having hardly slept at all. His collarbone twinged and ached as if a hurricane with his name on it was waltzing its way across Texas. His mama had once cautioned to listen to that busted bone because in addition to weather forecasting it was also gauging the stress level in his life. If that was true he was in for a painful summer since he'd just bitten off a whole new chunk of responsibility.

While he shaved and dressed in casual clothes, he pondered and prayed over yesterday's brief discovery of Ali with those kids who were tattooed like gang members. There had to be a reason for why she'd hang out with people of their ilk, but she hadn't offered it even when he'd mentioned the park in hopes that she'd explain. She hadn't opened up—if anything she'd clammed up. He'd tossed all night, wondering how it would feel to truly have Ali's trust and respect. This morning as he drove to the campus he was no closer to knowing.

On the flip side, Ben was in a continual stage of praise that Ethan seemed to have settled into a stable place. He still spent ninety percent of his time in his room, but he was willing to get out of the house for short periods if it meant seeing Ali and Simba. They were a miracle drug, a tonic for the sadness that had hung over the Lamar house for far too long.

Because of Ali, the throbbing in Ben's shoulder couldn't hold a candle to the ache in his chest. He missed her presence in his home. Missed her wisdom, her wit and her compassion for others. Quite simply, he missed the confident woman who had stolen his heart.

Will Ali ever love me the same in return, Father? Please give me some encouragement today. I need something positive to hold on to.

With his silent prayer ended Ben waved his hand before Ethan's face to get his attention. Ethan clicked off the iPod and tugged the earphones free. Today he was looking every bit a normal, handsome fifteen year old who needed a haircut. The occasion of visiting the geologic exhibit had him pushing past his anxiety, just as Ali had said he could if he wanted to exercise control over his many fears.

"There they are!" Ethan's spotted Ali and Simba waiting beneath the tall, white portico. Though his excitement was contagious, Ben didn't need any provocation to be jazzed about the next few hours. He didn't even mind that the dog was tagging along. Maybe he'd try brushing the back of his hand against her sleek coat when nobody was looking. Maybe.

Ethan allowed his father to hand him the backpack filled with comfort items. He tucked his iPod inside and double-checked each compartment, methodically keeping track as he unzipped and zipped, unzipped and zipped each pocket multiple times. Being an Asperger sufferer meant self-soothing through rituals of counting and touch. So, bringing along personal items or a few favorite rock specimens would help if anxiety began to invade.

Ben looked toward Ali, standing patiently only twenty yards away. But even that short distance was too far. He wanted her close. He thought back to the near-kiss as she'd slept on his sofa, wished he'd taken advantage of that private moment but fearing her reaction if she'd awakened. Ben was magnetically drawn to her, sensed she cared as well, even though she hadn't made any romantic overtures. But there were a number of clues that made him suspect a strong reason existed in her past for her reservations.

Ali had become like a big sister to Ethan, if not a mother figure. She was having a huge impact, teaching him how to manage his behavior. Ben was reluctant to mess with what was working to satisfy his own selfish needs, but the more he knew of the woman the more he wanted to know. If only she'd volunteer the dark details he didn't dare ask for.

"Happy Memorial Day!" She called, waving a small American flag, the classic red white and blue colors matching her plaid knee-length shorts and the bandana tied around Simba's neck.

Ethan hoisted the straps of his bag over his shoulders and fell into step as they crossed the short space to Ali.

"What's the big deal about this holiday?" Ethan grumbled.

"Good morning, sunshine." Ali poked at his

usual grumpy state. "The big deal of Memorial Day is honoring the brave people who fought and died for this country. Their sacrifice allows you the freedom to be here today."

"No, my dad's connections allow us to be here today when the place is closed."

Ali propped one fist on her hip and pointed the flag at him in warning. "I know your world is comfortably small, Ethan, but stretch your mind to a grander scale just for a minute if that's possible. If not for the brave men and women who've given their lives, you could be speaking a different language and pledging allegiance to a flag that doesn't approve of the liberty we enjoy. And that, kiddo, is the big deal about this holiday. You got it?"

"Got it." His eyes were downcast for a moment while he let Simba sniff his hand. "Sorry."

The voluntary apology sent a wide-eyed glance between Ali and Ben.

"You're forgiven." She affirmed his effort. "Shall we go inside?" Ali swept her hand toward the entrance where the security guard waited to unlock the door.

Ben's chest swelled to bursting beneath his shirt, filled with pride for Ali and the way she handled his son's disrespectful moment. Without thinking twice he draped an arm around her shoulders as they headed for the door.

"Score one for the Rock." Ben murmured close to her ear as he gave her shoulders a squeeze, wanting so much to embrace her. To kiss her.

"You think?" She looked up, her face so near, her skin so fair and lovely, her lips so inviting.

He forced a chuckle, afraid his thoughts would otherwise give him away. "Absolutely. I've all but given up on confronting his nasty comments, partly because we'd be at each other's throats all the time and partly because I know he's not always aware of how rude he sounds."

"And that's why you're going to be the good cop to my bad cop," she explained. "Let me be the heavy when we're together and eventually Ethan will pick up on the words and behaviors that get his ears pinned back. If he wants me to keep coming around he'll have to adjust his style."

Ben couldn't help wondering if that guidance applied to him as well.

Ali wiggled out from under his arm, stepped back and stared up into his face. "Those are some pretty big bags you're packin'." She gestured toward the dark circles he'd noted in the bathroom mirror.

"And I thought I was home free when Ethan didn't point it out."

She offered up a sheepish grin and a shrug before adding, "Hey, you're about to step back into the public's brutally critical eye. You've gotta keep your game face on and be lookin' good. I bet Laura Epps isn't missing her beauty rest, so what's up? You've made your decision, so why aren't you sleeping like a newborn babe?"

Lord, is this You giving me another opportunity to question her about yesterday? Ben couldn't be sure and he didn't want to spoil a special day that was just getting started.

"I guess I underestimated how much there would be to decide right out of the chute. When Randy is on a mission there's little that slows him down, including the clock." It was true, just not the whole truth. "He phoned late last night with a list of things to consider. And he gave me a wakeup call this morning wanting answers."

"You sure you're up for this tour today?" Her narrow auburn brows tilted together in concern. "It's gonna be very exciting, you know. Paleozoic rocks are well represented in Texas and we are about to be treated to some rare vertebrate shark fossils on display from the Permian period."

He closed his eyes, shook his head. "Where did that spiel come from?"

Ali fished into her bag and produced a page that looked to be printed from some website. "While you were considering your buddy's questions all night I was surfing the Paleontology Portal."

"Sounds like party time."

"It was a struggle but I held my excitement in check, which is why I look well rested."

"Y'all come on!" Ethan called from inside the building. The guard held the door open, tapped his toe and waited for them to follow.

"Shall we?" Ben offered Ali his arm.

"By all means." She curled her fingers around his biceps and gave a gentle squeeze. Ben felt the pressure all the way to his heart.

"Are you sure we should be doing this?" Ali waited for Simba to jump to the ground and then slammed the vehicle door.

"Is there anything illegal or immoral about

two single adults digging in the flower bed?"
Ben asked.

"Not the last time I checked. But one of those
adults is about to put his name on a hotly con-
tested ballot and doesn't need any wagging
tongues over his personal life."

Ali preceded him through the door Ethan
had left wide open in his haste to get upstairs
and crash. Ben couldn't remember the last time
he'd seen his son worn out to the point of exhaustion, but the day had been more demanding of the boy physically and emotionally than
they could have expected. In a good way.

"There's fresh lemonade in the fridge.
Would you bring a couple of glasses out back
for us, please?" Ben headed straight through
the family room, out the sliding doors and
down the steep flight of steps to the pool and
dining area. He dropped a country CD into the
outdoor sound system and sang along with his
favorite troubadour while he rolled a wheelbar-
row full of gardening supplies from the potting
shed. As he passed the pool Ben could see Ali
making herself at home in the kitchen.

Warmth coursed through his veins at the
sight of her moving about his familiar rooms as
if she belonged. It had been years since he'd felt

complete in his own home. Ali was the missing piece. She was making them whole again.

Oh, Father, give me patience and wisdom to take this slowly when what I really want to do is sweep this amazing woman off her feet.

Ben laughed out loud at the thought. She'd been keeping an eye on him from the first moment they'd met. There was little chance she'd be taken by surprise, much less swept off her feet. Everything Ali did was deliberate, well thought out and prayerfully planned.

Which reminded him again of the previous day's discovery. He should have revealed himself, but he'd hurried away. Now, how could he reconcile these two sides of Ali? The one secretive, keeping questionable company under wraps and the other a direct, in-your-face therapist who was making such headway with Ethan?

"Can I bring anything else?" she called from the balcony.

He pushed aside the disturbing thoughts and focused on the charming lady one flight up. "Actually, wait there and you can help me gather up everything so we'll be ready to grill later."

He took the white limestone steps two at a time, feeling adrenaline surge as he climbed higher. Recognizing the increase in his pulse as he drew closer.

Closer to the woman who'd become the center of his world.

He reached the landing, stepped through the sliding door, slapped his hands and rubbed them together.

"Okay, let me get the meat seasoned and back into the cooler and then we'll go get elbow deep in dirt." He poked his head into the fridge and busied himself with a package of ground sirloin when what he really wanted to do was take Ali in his arms and confess his feelings.

I have to get my imagination under control. I haven't been this jittery since my last NFL game.

Remembering the teak serving tray he'd bought for outdoor use he closed the stainless steel door, turned about face and stepped right into Ali's arms.

Chapter Eighteen

Ali slid trembling hands around Benjamin's taut waist, tipped her head back and forced a smile. This was a meant-to-be moment and she was grabbing it and the man she loved with all her might. She'd never had the inclination or the courage to be so forward and might not get a chance like this again.

Heavenly Father, don't let me make a fool of myself. If Benjamin isn't seriously interested please let the floor open up and swallow me whole!

Ali pressed her palms against the firmness of Benjamin's back, dared to pull him closer, kept her gaze fixed on the deepest blue eyes she'd ever seen. She drew in a breath while she tried to think of something clever to say, something that would make this obvious overture seem accidental. She closed her eyes, praying that when she opened them he'd look a little less stunned and maybe return her smile.

In the quiet of the kitchen, with George Strait crooning in the distance, she felt the motion of Benjamin bending toward her as he wrapped her in his arms and pressed her close. A physical peace she'd never known washed over her spirit.

His lips smothered her mouth, softly. His hands spread wide, one above the other supporting her spine, sweeping her backward as if to dip her low in a wedding day waltz. Ali clasped her hands behind his neck, feeling the pulse in his throat thumping in time with the heartbeat pressed close to her own. His kiss took possession of her lips and her soul. She was helpless and hopeless, swept away by Benjamin's presence.

Far too soon he raised her upright and set her securely on her feet before releasing her from his arms.

"Thank you," she murmured. She cast her gaze downward for fear of what she might learn from the expression on his face.

He pressed a knuckle beneath her chin, forced her eyes to meet his. "Thanks for what?"

"For not letting me feel like the Lone Ranger over that impetuous hug."

"Impetuous? So, when you slid your arms around my body you had no intention of letting me kiss you?"

"Well, I, uh…" She stammered for an answer, tried to turn away. Benjamin caught her by the wrist and pulled her close. Pinned her once again to his solid chest.

"Let me tell you what I learned from watching my parents. When my mama cozied up to my daddy in the kitchen, she was either looking for a kiss or a credit card. You don't seem like the outlet mall type so I figured some smoochin' might be in order."

"Smoochin'? I haven't heard anybody use that term in a month of Sundays. That's funny."

Benjamin brought his face so close the tip of his nose touched Ali's.

"Then how come I don't hear you laughin'?" he murmured, his lips pressing hers lightly so she felt as much as heard the question.

If he expected an answer he didn't give her a chance to offer one. Instead he claimed her mouth again, this time more insistent than the last. She could count the number of men she'd allowed to kiss her on two fingers and none had come close to turning her head. Benjamin had it spinning and she held on for dear life.

They called her the Rock. Solid and calm, unchanging in the storm. But at this moment, right now, a tempest stirred in her core. And just when she felt her knees would go weak, he exercised the wisdom of Solomon by ending the intimate moment, releasing her from the embrace and stepping back a few inches. He smoothed stray hairs away from her face and ran the tips of his fingers down one side of her jaw.

"I'm tempted to say you're beautiful, but that's not the right word to describe you."

"Maybe because it's a little too classy for me." She tried to joke, never having thought of herself in that way. She'd always been proud of her strength of character, which she felt attracted people to her. But not so much with physical appearance since she'd never even come close to the svelte women in the fashion magazines.

The lines between his sandy brows deepened as a frown carved a bracket around his mouth. "If anything it's too common. You're a tempting and complicated woman, Ali."

She huffed, the slightest sound of disbelief at his comment. His scowl deepened.

"Believe it or not, I understand that reaction." He nodded. "I always felt people were drawn to me because of my athletic success. I was at the end of my football career before I recognized that being a Dallas Cowboys linebacker wasn't the only reason people cared about me. I learned that my value was as much for encouraging words as it was for reading an offensive line. It's about who I am, not what I do. Just as it is with you, my love."

She felt a buzz of connection as if someone had thrown a switch, freeing a powerful current to flow between the two of them. She longed to articulate the newfound feelings, but his use of the endearment blurred her thoughts, made them too confusing. She didn't dare to interpret him literally. So, she kept the moment light.

"Is that your way of saying I'm not just a pretty face?"

"Exactly!" He exclaimed. "I'm more than a big ole meat-headed, no-necked monster of a football player. And you're so much more than the doctor who listens to the problems of mixed-up kids and hangs from helicopters in an orange jumpsuit. It's who you are in here that has me falling in love with you, Ali."

He tapped his index finger on the center of her chest, not knowing how his words and that light touch stirred the pain she'd carried deep inside for as long as she could remember. Maybe it was time to let the pain go.

Ben's heart rattled against his ribs, a creature determined to break loose from its cage now that the truth had set it free.

Lord, I beg You, let her feel the same!

As silent pleas rose heavenward, he watched the enchanting pink flush in Ali's cheeks spread to her hairline. Ben thought he knew all about women, but he'd started back at square one the day she'd air dropped into his life and then promptly stomped out of it.

She had a great deal to give and he had so much to learn. How would he ever experience it all when he'd just tied the mantle of politics like a millstone around his neck and then dived for the deepest channel in the sea?

He couldn't even be sure of her vote, so how could he expect to know what she felt in the depths of her heart?

"Is there any chance you're confusing gratitude with love?" she asked, her voice low to soften the impact of her words.

"Whoa, that response is not what I had in mind." The question took him aback.

"What did you expect me to say?"

"Well, when a man lays his soul bare right in the middle of the kitchen he's usually hoping for some sort of positive reinforcement."

"Then let me put it another way. If you saved a stranger from a burning building and they pledged undying loyalty to you, how would you ever know if that gift came from the person's heart or from their sense of obligation? And what if you'd simply been doing your job and didn't deserve the loyalty?"

Ben shoved both hands through his hair and kept his fingers laced behind his head while he considered what she'd said.

"Let me see if I understand you correctly. You're wondering if what I'm feeling for you is really just gratitude because you've helped me with Ethan."

She nodded. "It wouldn't be the first time thankfulness was twisted into something more. It's a potent emotion."

He massaged the back of his skull, counted to ten and then placed his hands on Ali's shoulders. Leaning in he fixed his gaze on hers.

"Once again, I understand where you're

coming from. I didn't expect it and don't like it, but I understand. People do sometimes get their emotions fouled up with their motives. But I promise you, sweet lady, that's not the case with me. I may be out of practice expressing it, but I haven't forgotten what the real deal should feel like."

He pulled Ali to him, folded her close and tucked her head beneath his chin. "This ain't gratitude, Ali. This is love. If you don't return it I can deal with that. But please don't sell yourself short by thinking you don't deserve this."

Her head bobbed but she didn't speak. He felt her chest expand with a big breath and wondered if she was taking in his words or letting them spill over the dam that was built around her emotions. He inhaled her sweet scent, planted a tender kiss on the top of her auburn head and let his arms slide to his sides.

"Okay, then." He turned away to find some busy work, anything to hide his disappointment. He pulled open the storage closet and located the large serving tray. Plopping it onto the counter he began to load it with tall plastic glasses and the pitcher of iced lemonade. "While I take this outside and get started digging up that bed would you mind checking on Ethan? I doubt he'll have the energy to come back down but it's worth a try."

"Sure, I'd be happy to." She turned toward the door that would take her through the foyer, across the family room and upstairs to Ethan's suite. As she put several steps between them, he couldn't help admiring the curves of her body and the honesty of the spirit he suspected carried a deep wound.

"Benjamin?" She'd turned back to face him. "No one's ever said those things to me. It means a lot."

He gave her a small smile, unable to push more words past the tightness in his throat. He'd offered her his love and she'd given him back what she believed he felt. Gratitude. There was much more to Ali than he knew.

More than he'd ever know unless she'd trust him enough to tell him the secret she held onto so tightly.

"Simba, come." Ali gave a hand signal as she put her foot on the first step. Simba stood but didn't follow. Instead she turned her long, regal nose toward the kitchen, her ears crooked in the direction of Benjamin. When she looked back again she tilted her head, judgment in those dark eyes. Ali signaled again, *come*. Simba dropped down to the carpet, put her nose on her paws and blew out a puff of breath, a doggie sigh if ever there was one.

"Suit yourself, traitor," Ali murmured, then headed up the steps.

As she dragged one foot higher than the other she bit back the trembling that threatened to overtake her lips. Lips Benjamin has just kissed. He'd said the things she'd dreamed of hearing and she'd dismissed them.

Dismissed them to his face.

But it was the right thing to do. He was going places she didn't want to go, would stand for causes she might not agree with, needed a mother for his son even more than a helpmate for himself.

And then there was that family history, that name he was so proud of. Ali couldn't fit into his life in a million years, and she prayed he'd never have to know why.

She rapped lightly on Ethan's doorframe, expecting he might be asleep.

"What?" he blurted. Ethan reclined face-down across his bed, still fully dressed including scuffed and dirty hightops.

"Is that any way to speak to me after the

awesome day we've had?" She moved into his room and took her usual seat at his desk.

"Are you in love with my dad?" Ethan mumbled, his mouth pressed against the bed covers.

"Oh, good grief." Ali refused to let the renewed hammering in her chest be her primary concern just now. "What is it with the Lamar men today?"

"It's okay with me if you are. Not that anybody cares what I think." He grudgingly gave his blessing.

Ali stared at the top of Ethan's rumpled head, wondering what was prompting this and where it was leading. Though he'd shown improvement, it was still early. She knew only too well that tragedy could snuff out progress in the blink of an eye. Ali left the chair, moved across the room and risked perching on the corner of Ethan's king-size mattress.

"Your feelings are very important, and if there was anything between your dad and me you'd be the first to know about it."

Had the boy come down the stairs and seen them together in the kitchen? Ali mentally flinched at the thought of what Ethan might have witnessed. And if he had seen something, was he interpreting it through the lens of his teenage mind or the perspective of his childish thinking?

Ethan raised his head off the blanket. The eyes he'd inherited from his father gave her a mocking glare.

"Don't patronize me, Ali. I'm mentally ill but I'm not blind or stupid."

"Very well said. Please continue."

He pushed upright and flopped into a cross-legged sitting position. "This was supposed to be *my* day. At least you made an effort to know what the exhibit was about, but Dad couldn't have cared less so he should have stayed home. The way you two ignored me I might as well have been there by myself."

"Ethan, we were within six feet of you all day long. I intentionally took you on a holiday when the library was closed so you could enjoy the fossils without being disturbed by other people. I left you alone so you could concentrate."

"You left me alone so you could concentrate on my dad."

Ethan's accusation was like a hard landing that knocks the breath out of you, and a body slam like that was usually your own fault for not paying attention to your boundaries. Did she deserve the blow he'd just dealt her?

"You made dreamy eyes at him like the women who come up and ask for his autograph."

"Ethan, if I gave that impression it was inappropriate and I apologize." Was she so pathetically transparent?

"It wasn't all your fault." He flapped a hand at her apology. "Dad was watching you like a hungry mockingbird watches a fat worm."

She couldn't resist snickering at the metaphor.

Ethan's mouth twisted in a sly grin. "That's one Dad says all the time I was just looking for a chance to use it."

"Well, you did good." She risked laying a hand on his knee. "I really am sorry if I didn't pay enough attention to you today. My effort to give you some personal space was well intentioned. I certainly never expected that your dad and I would get distracted by each other's company."

Ethan nodded but slid his legs straight out on the bed, scooting away from her touch.

"If you're willing to go when the place is full of people we'll try again another day."

"Just you and me?" His voice was hopeful.

"No, your father needs to be there, too."

"But why?" he whined.

"Ethan, I'm only your therapist, somebody who will be here for as long as you need me. But your dad is your family, and he'll be here for you forever. You have to work your problems and differences out between the two of you. I'm not the mediator or the glue that keeps you working together." *And I never can be.*

"So, what are you telling me?"

Simple question. Difficult answer. It was time to see if he could handle it.

"Honey, I'm not a substitute for your mama."

"But if you would try to be then maybe Dad could forgive me."

"Forgive you for what?"

Ethan's normally expressionless, stony face crumbled, like a mask of molded clay deprived of water for too long.

"She had the accident because of me," he confessed, his voice just above a whisper. "It was raining hard but I kept talking. She asked me to let her pay attention to the road but I wouldn't shut up. When the other car cut us off she was distracted by my big mouth. It's my fault she died."

"No it's not, kiddo. Blaming ourselves won't change tragic things. Taking on guilt doesn't undo the past or serve any useful purpose. Believe me, I know."

He slung his long legs to the side of his bed

and stood, then moved as if heading toward the dressing room for privacy. But three steps from Ali he stopped, turned about face and dropped to his knees on the floor at her feet. The boy so adverse to physical contact and displays of emotion buried his face in Ali's lap, wrapped his arms around her waist and cried as if his life was over. His tears flowed freely for the loss of his mother, the loss of his innocence, the loss of his hope.

Ali stroked Ethan's head and wept along with him for all the same reasons.

Chapter Nineteen

When she'd dried the last of her tears and Ethan's hiccups had subsided, Ali patted his back lightly and suggested they go outside and enjoy what was left of the beautiful afternoon.

"The sooner I help your dad dig up that flower bed the sooner he can grill us a burger. I noticed enough ground beef in the fridge to feed the Aggie Corps of Cadets."

Ethan rocked back on his haunches, grabbed the edge of his covers and wiped his nose on the sheet. Ali made note to leave a reminder for the housekeeper to change the linens.

"You won't tell Dad about this, will you?"

"Not as long as you come down and visit with us."

He squinted through still-shiny eyes and

tilted his head to stare just like Simba had done earlier. "That's blackmail."

"Yeah, I know."

"Does the term 'self-sabotage' ring a bell with you, big sister?" Erin's reaction to Ali's retelling of the day's events was much stronger than expected. It probably would have been better to wait until after the ride home, but Ali had phoned as soon as she'd hit the highway.

"I prefer to think of it as brutal honesty."

"To what end, may I ask? What is the point in offending a guy who's declared his love unless it's to run him off so you won't have to deal with your feelings?"

"For a civilian, you're pretty savvy about psychoanalysis."

"If savvy is learning from my own experience, then I guess that's what I am. Mostly I just decided to quit letting fear set up a roadblock between me and happiness. The only way I could do that was to stop running from Daniel and Dana and let them teach me how to be part of a loving family."

A loving family. That was a fantasyland Ali and her siblings had never visited. Their home was a place for survival, not bonding, and life in foster care hadn't been much better. As adults they'd compensated in different ways—Erin by abandoning her husband and child, Ali through studying the dysfunction caused by abuse. And since Heath wouldn't answer her letters, it was anybody's guess how their little brother had come to cope with their violent childhood.

"Alison, listen to me. Ben Lamar is a decent guy who's fallen in love with you for all the right reasons. Don't let the differences in who you are and how you grew up keep you from the life God wants you to have. He's sent a Christian man to cherish you. Don't throw that back in His face."

Ali made the rest of the drive to her townhouse in silence, not even turning on the radio for company. Occasionally she glanced back at Simba, who'd refused the rare offer to ride up front with her harness secured to the seatbelt. Instead, she'd waited stubbornly at the back gate of the Land Rover as if to say her crate was preferable to being an arm's length from her mixed-up mistress.

The last of the sun's red-orange rays had bled out of the night sky and a brilliant canopy of stars was beginning to sparkle in the distance. The tangy lemonade in her to-go cup was difficult to swallow past the emotions in her throat that had become a knot in her chest. A knot of guilt that wouldn't serve any useful purpose, just as she'd told Ethan.

Father, if a boy with Asperger's can wrap his damaged mind around that concept, why can't I? Please, Lord, help me push past this fear just like my sister's done. I want to be part of a family, too.

And this time Ali hoped it would be forever.

The day of the Rescue Round Up began with a flurry of butterflies so intense Ali could hardly keep her oatmeal down. The skies above San Angelo, famous for being clear and endlessly high, were dotted with fat gray clouds floating ominously low. A blowing rain would add an unexpected dimension to the day's competition. It might slow her down but it sure wouldn't shut her down.

Sporting their colors, she and Simba loped across the field toward the area staged for the annual smackdown. Each year's obstacle course was more demanding than the last, the evil architects determined their designs would get the best of the contestants.

"Holy smoke!" She came to a stop beside

her teammates, equally conspicuous in bright orange. Ali joined them in surveying the temporary network of walls, trenches, tunnels, rope swings and mud pits extending across a hundred-yard stretch of county-donated space.

"Is this thing meant to challenge us or kill us?"

"Yeah, that's pretty much how we reacted." Harry slung an arm around her neck, gave her a quick squeeze and added a brotherly brush of knuckles to her crown intended to muss up whatever efforts she'd made toward a tight braid.

"Now I'm really glad the guys at Lackland Air Force Base invited us to come out and test their equipment last fall."

Sid threw back his head and brayed like a nervous donkey.

"What's up with him?" She looked to Harry for an explanation.

"Darlin', I'm afraid the joke's on us. That *invitation* to Lackland was a setup to see just how much old coots like me and Sid could take. The same guys who built that course put this one up and they can't wait to see us crash and burn."

"Not if I have anything to say about it," Ali boasted for the sake of her teammates. If she caved in to intimidation at 7:00 a.m. it wouldn't bode well for the rest of the morning.

"Take it easy on this thing, lady. Don't try to set any records—just get to the end. You mastering the Sears Tower over there counts for a whole lot more team points than your time on this relay."

"Sears Tower, huh?" She craned her neck to spot it.

Sid pointed. "It's on the far side of these pines. At least a hundred feet, *straight up*."

"Cool!" Ali felt a grin of anticipation spread across her face. The climb and rappel was her forté, and the higher the better. Making her way up a sheer piece of rock and then the flutter back down to earth was second nature, but she still experienced an icy shiver of anticipation before each ascent.

"Did you hear him?" Harry asked. "A hundred feet!" He twisted his weathered face into a silly caricature of trepidation. Ali knew part of it was for real.

"Not to worry, my friend. Just make it as high as you can and leave planting the flag to me," she reassured her partner. Height had never bothered her. Where these guys favored the inside of the chopper, she preferred to hang from the long line where the three hundred sixty-degree view was unobstructed.

"Let's go take a look and get registered." She glanced up at the dark clouds and then toward the empty bleachers where only a couple dozen folks sat beneath bright umbrellas or dressed in yellow rain slickers.

"From the looks of this sky I'm thinking we won't have many witnesses if we blow it."

"Your cheering section is already here." Harry winked.

"Cheering section?" She played dumb but couldn't keep her hand from pressing her stomach to quiet the somersaults it was turning.

"Come ooooooon. Did you think you were gonna get off scot-free?" Harry looked to Sid who nodded agreement. "We know Ben Lamar's sweet on you and don't even bother to deny it because why else would the man and his kid be out here on a day like this? It sure ain't for a game of touch football. So mosey on over there, say 'hello' and ask him real nice like for an autograph for me. I've kicked myself a hundred times for not doing it the day we pulled his boy out of Big Bend."

Her spirit danced a highland jig. *Benjamin's here.*

They hadn't had a reason to speak since Monday and she didn't think there was any chance he and Ethan would show up. Why did she continually underestimate the guy?

Because if you don't trust him completely, he can't yank the rug out from under you.

Could Erin be right about the self-sabotage?

"So, what's it gonna be?" Harry pushed. "I'll trade you a flight lesson for the autograph."

"Make it two lessons or I'll tell the captain you're using department equipment for personal gain."

"Hey, that's blackmail."

"Yeah, I know. It seems to be working well for me lately."

Ben spotted Ali several minutes before she headed their direction. It was all he could do not to meet her halfway and give her a kiss for good luck. In truth that would only be an excuse to feel her in his arms again.

"Here they come!" Ethan was constantly on the verge of an outburst when it came to Ali and Simba. It was so nice to see his kid excited about something besides Jurassic core samples.

Ben resisted the urge to match Ethan's fidgety behavior, a test of strength since he was as nervous inside as a bridegroom on his wedding day. The comparison was ironic considering that the woman striding his way had all but rejected his heart, chalking his feelings up to gratitude.

In the hours since he'd seen her last, the Holy Spirit had led Ben to seek scriptures on the emotion the Bible mentioned so often. Ben was reminded that love is greater than faith, greater than hope. Love bears all things. Love does not keep a record of wrongs. Love endures forever.

Yes, Ben was indebted to Ali for the patience and understanding she'd shown Ethan and for the improvements he'd experienced since she'd come into their lives. And Ben was appreciative of her blunt honesty. It had helped him make more than one important decision regarding the campaign. But if all that had never happened, if there had been no progress whatsoever, Ben was certain he'd still have this undeniable, gravitational pull toward Alison Stone.

He was compelled to have her in his life. Not just as a friend and certainly not simply as a voter.

How can I make her understand this tidal wave of love, this river of tenderness that's flowing through me? I barely comprehend it myself.

She came to a stop three rows below them at the bottom of the bleachers. Her smile was for Ethan but Ben felt it splash against him like the fat drops that had begun to fall.

"How nice of y'all to brave the elements today." She did an exaggerated double take, then made zero effort to hide her amusement. "I dig the fashion statement. You two look like the guys on the box of frozen fish at the grocery store."

"I told Dad that, but he wouldn't listen." Ethan complained for the umpteenth time since Ben had handed his son the yellow rain gear in the parking lot and insisted he step into the plastic pants and hooded jacket.

"Thanks a lot," Ben mouthed. Ali shrugged, no sign of apology in eyes that were free of mascara.

"You look strange." Ethan stared, trying to figure it out.

"Strange better?" Ali tossed him a high one.

"Just strange." A swing and a miss.

Ben laughed, shook his head, glad she wasn't easily offended. "I like it. It's a nice look for you." He drew an imaginary circle around his face indicating her lack of makeup.

"Cosmetics are a waste of time on a day like today. Between the rain, the sweat and the mud there's not much point in the effort. Eyeliner will turn me into a raccoon and lipstick will end up on my teeth or my sleeve. So I opted for a natural face that only needs a garden hose to freshen up."

"Are you really gonna do that?" Ethan pointed to the obstacle course.

"Sure am. I'm the second leg of the relay and I have to move as fast as I can so my team will score a good time."

"And what about that thing?" He shielded his eyes, tipped his head back and looked toward the top of the portable rock wall.

"That *thing* is my specialty. That's why I was able to get down the cliff when you were trapped in Big Bend."

"I wasn't trapped," he insisted.

"Okay, when you were hiding out in the bottom of a canyon with your foot wedged in a rock."

"That's more like it."

Ben was amazed at Ethan's effort to spar verbally with Ali. His son was experiencing success, a more powerful motivator than any drug his former doctors had prescribed.

"When to do I get my turn?" Ethan hadn't forgotten their deal.

"After the competition is over we all meet back here to help anybody who wants to try a couple of obstacles or take a shot at the climbing wall as long as the weather clears." Ali turned her face to Ben. "Or hug a dog for five minutes." She hadn't forgotten either.

Ben looked toward the canine he'd come to realize was extremely intelligent. Simba was watching him, an interesting gleam in her eyes. Could it be compassion? Nope, more likely a taunt.

"Don't get hurt," Ethan cautioned, another indicator he was thinking beyond himself.

"I was about to say the same thing," Ben added, his gaze once again resting on Ali. He stood and descended the bleachers to stand toe to toe with her. Though they'd been apart she'd never left his mind. He'd been praying all week for the Lord to keep her safe. He glanced toward the field where the competitors were stretching and warming up.

"Now that I've seen these torture devices y'all call obstacles I have to question the good sense of anybody who volunteers to do this stuff."

"Well, if that ain't the pot callin' the kettle black." Ali rested fists on both hips, a sure sign she was about to make an important point.

"I'm pretty sure you spent more than half your life being a crash test dummy on the football field. However, my opponent is the clock and not eleven guys in body armor with the number on my chest in their crosshairs."

"Point well taken," Ben gave into her logic.

"Yours is too. Trust me, I'm fond of my limbs, freckles and all. I'll take care not to break any of them."

He didn't ask for permission because she might not give it. Instead he bent close, encircled her body with his arms and pulled her into a hug for a quick prayer.

"Please keep your child safe, Lord. You're not the only one who loves her."

Ali returned the pressure of his embrace, resting her head against his chest a moment longer. Then she signaled Simba who dropped into step, obedient as always.

"Wish us luck," Ali called over her shoulder.

"Like the Rock's gonna need it," a female to Ben's left complained to her friend.

He pretended not to hear the comment, dropping to adjust the lace on his sneaker in case she said more, which she did.

"Can you believe my bad fortune?" the woman whined.

"Oh, Hannah, it's not the Olympics. Today is just supposed to be for fun."

"I know, but I had a hard time making the El Paso team and with this being my first Round Up I was hoping to draw somebody a little closer to my ability."

"You definitely got a tough break pulling Alison Stone for the climb. But take it one inch at a time and do your best, Hannah. If you don't make it to the top it won't be the end of the world."

"No, but it might be the end of my rescue career. If a woman can't hold her own during these games the guys sure don't want you covering their backs in a crisis. To the Rock this may only be for braggin' rights, but it's a do-or-die event for me."

The blast of a warning whistle from the direction of the field ended the conversation. The girl named Hannah took off in a run, a trim figure in royal blue heading toward the starting line of the obstacle course. Her female friend took a seat several rows above Ethan. As Ben climbed to his spot the woman gave him a long look. From the crease of suspicion between her eyes he knew the scrutiny had nothing to do with being a former Dallas Cowboy or a candidate for Congress. Her perusal had everything to do with his being a fan of the woman they revered.

Alison Stone. The Rock.

Chapter Twenty

Two hours later Ali felt like one of those mud creatures at the Renaissance Faire. Several tumbles during her leg of the relay left Ali filthy, limping and behind in the point count. She might be able to climb a smooth cliff like a tarantula but when it came to her ability to shimmy up a rope in pouring rain or duck-walk through a low tunnel flowing with two inches of water, her thunder thighs would forever be a liability.

She was reminded a dozen times during the race that her upper-body strength was not sufficient to offset the weight of the cellulite stubbornly clinging to the muscles below her waist.

The heavy rain finally passed them by and now all that remained was a steady drizzle that wasn't enough to wash away the crud clinging to her water-resistant clothing and exposed flesh. Knowing the man she loved was watching, Ali couldn't help but feel a bit self-conscious about her bedraggled appearance. She was far from vain, but come on, a lady in her late thirties still had plenty of pride.

She dutifully shook hands with her opponent, a slender young woman dressed in that incredible shade of royal blue that flatters every skin tone. The girl had either drawn a pass or her teammates had elected not to include her in the relay because she was still clean, dry and annoyingly gorgeous. By comparison Ali was a frump, so she moved away as soon as introductions were made.

"Who's this Hannah Cerasoli kid?" Ali whispered to Harry as he attached the safety line to her climbing harness.

"She's a newbie with the El Paso unit. Right outta college and about to get her first public whuppin'."

Ali groaned at the news.

"What?"

"Not only a rookie, but a baby rookie at that," she huffed. "Couldn't they pair me with somebody who'd make this a fair fight? Now

I'm gonna seem like a show-off instead of an experienced climber out to beat my own time."

"Your reputation precedes you so enjoy the trip and don't worry about the perception on the ground. Just focus on the summit and let me guide you." Harry gave the harness a final check and the belay system a hard yank.

"You're good to go and I won't take my eyes off you. Show 'em why we call you the Rock." He planted a peck on her cheek and moved aside. As soon as she cleared the first six feet he'd step back into place as her belayer, the person on the ground responsible for the rope feed.

Ali said a quick prayer, took some deep breaths to steady her insides, squatted a few times to loosen up tight muscles, then spotted her first handhold and prepared to begin. She glanced right to her opponent, a few seconds behind in preparation. When the girl finally took her position she nodded at Ali.

Together they signaled, "Climb ready?"

"Climb on," came their belayers' response and the competition began.

Ali moved upward, hand over hand as she searched for a route, her feet following by instinct. She kept her eyes fixed on the surface beneath her gloved fingers, her mind laser focused on reaching a point one hundred feet above the ground. In the periphery of her vision she knew an opponent was nearby and in the distance there was cheering. But Ali was alert only to the sight of the next grip and the sound of her belayer's commands.

"Twenty feet, Rock," Harry called, giving her a height bearing.

Ali apologized to God for dissing her thighs earlier. Now she was grateful for the thick muscles that propelled her higher, making the climb less stressful for her shoulders.

"Forty feet, keep moving."

She heard a ragged intake of breath from the woman in blue, judged the sound to be at least ten feet below. Ali knew her time was excellent despite the slippery nature of the synthetic stone tower. As she closed on the next height marker a gasp from the spectators penetrated her thoughts.

"Sixty feet, Rock. Stay focused, keep climbing."

A cry of distress ended Ali's concentration. She turned her head away from the wall, glanced down and to the right. Twisted in her ropes, Hannah Cerasoli was in big trouble. She couldn't climb higher and beginning the rappel wasn't an option. Her belayer was giving instructions Hannah couldn't possibly follow, tangled as she was.

"Don't stop, Ali!" Harry shouted. "Get to the top and you can check her on the way down."

He was right to urge her onward—the girl wasn't going anywhere. But from the frantic look on her face Ali could see Hannah was about to panic. In the couple of minutes it would take to finish the climb and get back down to the girl, she could be in a full-blown anxiety attack.

"Give me some slack," Ali instructed. As soon as she felt Harry loosen his hold she began to traverse away from her climbing path, then down and across where Hannah was struggling to control breaths that were turning to gasps.

"Stay calm, Hannah. Use your training."

Ali reached the girl, placed a protective arm around her heaving shoulders. She kept her voice soft, not wanting others to hear. "Don't look up or down, just keep your eyes fixed on the tower. I know you're afraid, but if you don't moderate your breathing you're gonna hyperventilate."

"Not afraid," Hannah wheezed. "Asthma."

Ali narrowed her eyes, searched the color of Hannah's face and lips for critical signs. "You have an inhaler?"

She nodded. "Left sleeve. Zipper."

"Hold me steady, Harry," Ali shouted. She unzipped the pocket, pulled the purple inhaler free and held it to Hannah's mouth while she drew in the medication. Her breathing improved within seconds.

"Thank you, Father. You are a good God," Ali gave praise. Hannah nodded agreement.

"So sorry," she whispered.

"I'll lecture you about this another time," Ali warned, assuming the role of the troubled-kid magnet she'd always been. "Right now let's get you untangled and down from here."

"No!" Hannah insisted. "Help me to the top or I'll be off the team. Please, Rock," she pleaded.

Ali glanced at her watch. The record time she'd hoped to set had passed ninety seconds ago. She heaved a sigh. No reason to hurry now.

She made quick work with Hannah's snarled rope and gave thumbs up to her belayer who returned the gesture. The spectators and teams on the ground applauded but sounds of disappointed murmuring floated upward as they assumed the ascent was over.

"Pride can get people killed, Hannah.

Promise me you'll confide in your captain and make this right with your team."

"I promise." Her voice was shaky but strong, her eyes wide with sincerity.

"Alrighty, then." Ali gave the girl a smile of encouragement. "Let's not waste this perfectly good adrenaline rush."

"Climb ready?" the two chorused.

"Climb on!"

The women resumed their upward motion and the small crowd below them erupted in cheers that continued until they planted their team flags at the summit.

"Dad!" Ethan threw his arms around Ben's neck for the first time in years. "Is Ali the coolest lady ever, or what?"

Unwilling to spoil the spontaneous moment, Ben remained passive, only giving Ethan a light pat on his back. The boy returned to excited clapping and cheering while Ben savored the *normalcy* of his son's behavior. It had to be further confirmation they'd be okay, that Ethan could weather whatever storms lay ahead.

"Why do you think she did that?" His eyes were wide and engaging as he waited for a response.

"Good question, son. What's your guess?"

Ethan, puzzled over the notion, then surprised Ben with a thoughtful answer. "Ali takes care of people. If she was OCD she'd be a compulsive helper."

"That's a perfect observation," Ben smiled his agreement, wondering if anybody would say the same of him. He was known as a "good guy," but a compulsive helper, probably not. The realization was a small hammer that began chipping away at his self-image. "I think Ali simply loves others more than she loves herself."

"Yep. And it's okay if we love her back, Dad."

A fresh gust of wind caught the tail of Ben's yellow slicker and slung clinging raindrops across his face, like chilly punctuation to Ethan's comment.

As the boy regularly noted, he was ill but not stupid.

"That's a very grown-up thing to say. Are you sure about that?" Ben's question was hopeful on many levels.

Ethan nodded. "Ali helped me see that feeling guilty about the past won't change what happened, and holding on to sad feelings might keep me from getting better. I promise to try harder, Dad. I want you to like me again."

"I love you, son." Ben fought to hold a powerful surge of emotions in check. Change of any kind had to come in very small doses with Ethan. A journey of a thousand miles began the same as a hundred-yard dash—one step at a time. Ethan had made the mental connection and the verbal commitment. With God's help the rest would follow.

"What are you two looking so serious about? Come down here and help us celebrate!"

The solemn look passing between father and son turned to joy at the sound of Ali's voice. As it had for weeks, her arrival made their happiness and their circle complete. The bleachers thundered beneath their feet until they reached the ground. Ben refused to hold back any longer. Words of love were out of the question in this public place, so he pulled her close, pressed her ear to his chest and let the beat of his heart speak for him.

She gave him a mighty squeeze and tilted her damp head up so their eyes could meet.

"Ali, what you did up there was one of the most unselfish acts I've ever witnessed on any playing field."

"Oh, you would have done the same thing."

"I don't think so." He chuckled. "In my sport

that would amount to giving possession of a fumbled ball back to the opposing quarterback and then escorting him into the end zone."

"Okay, maybe not." She laughed, a husky sound that never failed to make his pulse quicken. "What'd you think about all that?" She looked to Ethan.

"I think you were awesome and I want to try to climb the rope that dumped you on your tail end."

"Oh, don't remind me." She rubbed her backside. "My hardest fall of the day. I'm sure I knocked a couple of crowns loose when I hit that landing mat soaked with rain."

"Yeah, you should have seen how high the water flew up in the air. You're so heavy it looked like you did a cannonball."

Ali's exaggerated look of insult made Ethan give her a brief side squeeze before stepping away. Ben winked when she caught his eye. There was so much he wanted to tell her once they could be alone. And this time he wouldn't let her give him the brush off.

"Ethan, if you really want to try the rope climb we'll get you into a harness and you can give it a go." She turned to Ben. "You're gonna spot for him, okay?"

"I'll do my best if the Rock will agree to coach me and stick to us like glue."

"It's a deal."

Thirty minutes later Ethan had traded his yellow rain suit for a safety helmet and rigging. One of the rope specialists was giving final pointers. Ben hadn't felt such trepidation for his son since the day they took the training wheels off his bike and he promptly rode down the driveway, across the street and collided with the neighbor's Porsche. But Ali was close by with all the guidance they both needed. She wouldn't let them do anything dangerous.

"Excuse me, Mr. Lamar."

"Yes," Ben turned toward a young man with an expensive camera slung around his neck.

"I heard you're going to be running for Congress. I'm with the Young Republicans and it would be a coup to get this photo of you and your son up on my blog today. Would you mind, sir?"

The kid was nice enough to ask but such courtesy would be rare in the future. Ben had always been fair game for the press. Now, anytime he took Ethan out in public he'd be in the spotlight too.

Ben glanced toward Ali.

There was neither judgment nor encouragement on her face. She brought her shoulders to her ears, indicating it wasn't her decision to make.

A shrill beeping turned more heads her way.

"That's a 911 from dispatch. I've gotta go." She did a three hundred and sixty-degree pivot, obviously searching for her teammates.

"Wait!" Ethan cried. His face contorted, his eyes fearful, his alarm as real as it had been on the day Ben foolishly left his son at the camp in Big Bend. The outcome had been nearly disastrous and Ben's gut clenched at the reminder.

"I have to go. You two will be fine by yourselves."

"But you promised!"

"I promised to keep my end of the agreement and I have. Now you have to do your part, Ethan.

Her cell phone screeched again, she turned away.

"Ali, please." Ben needed her to stay, to see this effort through with Ethan who'd worked so hard all day, was making such incredible progress. Whether she would admit it or not, the three of them were becoming a family. "There are at least a hundred other rescue professionals out here today. Send somebody else. We can't do this without you."

She stepped close to keep their conversation private from the young reporter.

"I'm honored you feel so strongly, but it's simply not true. You and Ethan are father and son. It's time you started trusting one another instead of leaning on somebody else. You have big plans, places to go, things to do together and people wanting to take your picture. I'd say today is as good a day as any to get started."

She planted a quick smack on Ben's cheek and when she stepped back her eyes gleamed with that secret pain he'd seen a number of times before. Could it be that Ali's matter-of-fact words were as much to convince herself as they were to encourage Ben?

Without giving him the time to find out, she reached toward Ethan.

"You'll do great," she insisted. She wrapped her knuckles on his safety helmet. "Knock on wood!"

Chapter Twenty-One

Ali had been a rescue volunteer for six years, never second-guessing her priorities. During today's mission she gave one hundred percent of her physical ability, as always. But every little bit of her heart was somewhere else.

She'd warned Hannah that pride could cost lives, then turned around and drew on the same deadly sin.

Benjamin was right, someone else could have taken the call. But Ali was bent on making a point, if only to herself. She didn't belong in their lives—not on the personal level that seemed to be snowballing out of control. Benjamin and Ethan had to accept the truth and the sooner the better.

Ali was not in their league.

She wasn't self-deprecating; she just knew the facts. She could never have outrun her past so she'd used it instead to draw survivor strength. It made her a woman so certain of her convictions her friends called her the Rock.

But certainty wasn't always a good thing—in fact, this time it was tragic since she was certain she could never fit in with Ben's family or his plans. Her sense of decency would force her to confess her story and then he would look at her with disgust, agreeing it was best that she turn away before the tarnish on her past tainted his future.

As Ali drove the last mile to her home, the day's events replayed in her mind like an old-fashioned news reel. The excited faces of Ben and Ethan, the team's cheers during her muddy relay, Hannah's gratitude, the thankful smile of the accident victim during her airlift to the medical center.

God had been good. He'd given Ali more than she dreamed of, definitely more than she deserved. In response she found ways to bless her Sunday Kids, those who the Bible would call "the least of these."

Her life was full, she didn't dare want for more.

Ali pulled the Land Rover through the small

alley behind her townhouse complex and into her narrow, one-vehicle garage. She popped the back hatch, let Simba free from her travel crate and together they took the network of pathways to the local park for a short walk. Ali longed for a hot shower to remove the grit and grime that still clung to her skin. Then afterward she'd sit and talk with Josie. The two had reversed roles in recent days, with the young nursing student giving the doctor guidance counseling.

"Ali, wait up!"

She whipped about face to see Benjamin striding toward her, reminding her so much of the first day they'd met. What had only been a few weeks seemed like a lifetime. She felt more comfortable about the man as a candidate and her opinion of him as a parent had certainly changed. They'd come from such different worlds, but the world seemed a much smaller place now that she loved him.

"What are you doing here?" she asked, unable to pry her tired gaze from the picture he made: clean, dry, well dressed and as handsome as the Texas summer sky is high. From the crown of his sandy blond head to the leather soles of his expensive cowboy boots his demeanor promised "Vote for me. You won't be sorry!"

"I'm here to invite you to come home with us for dinner. We want to celebrate what God's done in our lives today."

"Tell me how Ethan did." While Simba sniffed about and stretched her legs Ali eased down to one of the slatted wooden benches to rest. When she swept an open hand toward the empty half of the bench, Benjamin joined her.

"My kid was amazing." He beamed with pride for his son.

Thank you, Father, for showing me how much this man loves his boy. It makes it so much clearer that I need to move on so they can get back to their own lives.

"Ali, I wish you'd been there to see how hard he worked to get up that rope."

"Did he make it?"

"Only about eight feet and even at that it took him a dozen times to get there." Benjamin's eyes crinkled at the edges as he recalled the image. "Ethan has a new appreciation for how hard your backside smacked that mat when you fell. I don't think he'll be making any more cannonball comments since he sent up more than a few sprays of water himself."

"And how about you, Dad? How long did it take to get over your case of nerves? I thought you were going to have a hissy fit when I had to leave."

The smile slipped off Benjamin's face. His temple throbbed as his jaw clenched to contain a thought that seemed to want out. Clearly she'd hit a raw nerve.

"Tell me what's on your mind," she encouraged him.

For a few moments he dipped his chin, then raised it again. An icy stare sliced the space between them, cut through her reserve.

"Are you asking as a doctor or a woman?"

"Whichever you prefer."

Ben's gut was sore from holding back emotion. For years he'd kept his feelings in check. He was calm for Theresa's sake when Ethan had been diagnosed. Then he was strong for Ethan when his mother had died. Since that time he'd remained steadfast and positive, certain God still had a plan for their lives, to give them a future and a hope. Ben was determined to wait on the Lord's timing even when his best friend cajoled, pestered and threatened. He'd wanted to cry out a thousand times at injustice, loss and insinuation but he'd kept it all inside. There were so many blessings in his life, he had no right to complain.

But now, to have the woman whose rejection that very morning was still fresh equate his agitation with a *hissy fit,* well that was simply more than a man should be expected to endure.

"Ali, I came here with the best of intentions. I meant to tell you what a wonderful day we had and to thank you for helping us move beyond the relational mess that had built up in our home."

"However..." She waited.

"However..." He paused, lowered his head to glance at his hands as they dangled between his knees. He should stop and pray, get his racing pulse under control, but the emotion wanted a voice, wouldn't wait another moment. He looked up.

"However, I'm really struggling with the fact that the woman I love will give so much of herself to others, to people who don't deserve her gifts, people who can't repay her kindness, people who will never be more than a drain on society. But she won't go into the emotional deep end with me. I just don't get it and I don't know how to deal with it." His inflection mirrored his mounting frustration.

Simba heard, stopped her sniffing and poking. She trotted over, stood next to his knee, closer than she'd ever been. She settled on her haunches at his feet, watching with the intensity that only another dog could possibly understand.

Ali's face was equally impassive, unreadable. Did she care at all? Had he gone too far or not far enough?

"Benjamin, I'm a bit confused because I don't know these people you refer to as *drains on society*. How about giving me a clue."

Guide my words, Lord. I have a feeling she's not going to take this well, but I need to get all the cards on the table.

"I saw you last Sunday." He hesitated, but knew he had to say the rest. "It was just for a few minutes. In the woods at Halfway Landing."

She leaned away as if she needed to put distance between them. *"You followed me?"* her voice was incredulous.

"No, that's not how it happened." He shook his head and held his palms outward to emphasize his innocence. "I met the folks from Lend a Hand out there to talk about some cooperation between their foundation and my campaign to help clean up that area. I wanted to see it firsthand, but I was warned about the no-accounts that hang out and leave a mess in the woods. I expected to find transients and un-desirables." He lifted both shoulders, lost for words. "But you, Ali? Why would you hang out with the very people who burden the city for tax dollars we can't afford and shouldn't need to spend? Why would you associate with such trash?"

The rush to judgment he'd meant to avoid went straight from his lips out into the world without benefit of first filtering through his good sense. The sound echoed in his ears about the same time Ali reacted to it. A sad smile curved her soft lips, she closed her eyes briefly, shook her head.

He knew that reaction. It was the spoken-just-like-a-stupid-man gesture. His goose was as good as cooked and any moment now she'd skewer him. But instead of unleashing fury, she seemed to accept his comment like an accurate indictment.

"Those *'undesirables'* are some of my *pro bono* clients from the homeless shelter. They would never get therapy otherwise. I call them my Sunday Kids because that's the only day of the week we get to spend time together."

He sucked in a breath, wishing it was as easy to suck back in the accusation. He'd known in his heart of hearts there was a reasonable answer, but she'd been so secretive.

"Are you trying to get them to go back to their parents where they belong?"

She laughed at the suggestion. The sort of brittle, nervous response a person has when they get a terminal diagnosis.

"Benjamin, being with a parent is not always the best place for a child. Those kids share a common experience that no one should have to endure."

"Physical abuse?"

"Worse." She breathed in deeply as if preparing for a revelation. "The worst, actually. Sexual abuse by a parent."

He flinched at the most perverse of behaviors, always having hoped there was a fiery reserved section in eternity for people who would injure a child, with a special hot seat for sexual predators.

"I'm sorry. I'd never have guessed."

"Most people wouldn't because they don't think twisted thoughts." Ali's chin dipped as she stared at her muddy boots. "It's the deepest, filthiest pit to climb out of for the few of us who make it."

"Don't you mean the few of *them?*"

"No. I mean *us.*" Amber eyes sought his. "You called them trash and many would agree. They're disposable, throw-away kids who've been used and forgotten. I spend my Sundays with them because I relate to what they couldn't escape, can't forget. I'm one of them, Benjamin."

"What?" He heard exactly what Ali said but didn't want to make sense of what she was telling him.

"My father began crawling into my bed when I was ten years old. He threatened to go to my little sister if I refused him. What else could I do?"

"You mean he…" Ben couldn't say the words.

"Yeah. Hard to believe a man would defile the very daughter God trusted him to love, isn't it?" Fat tears pooled in the corners of her eyes, slid beneath her lashes and dribbled down her mud-streaked cheeks.

"So, now you know my dirty little secret. That's the reason I could never be more to you than a paid employee. I don't deserve anything better."

A deep, deep sadness flooded Ben's soul as he grasped what Ali was telling him.

And suddenly Ethan's problems seemed small. He had family, friends, resources. He was loved and lovingly cared for in a world that held such low regard for the weak, for the least of these.

"I need some time to process what you've said. Will you please come back to the house with me?"

"Time won't make any difference. Trust me on this." She shook her head, wild strands of red wisped about her face. "I've used years of education and experience to try to make sense of what happened. I haven't been able to understand it, but the past molded me into who I am today. I learned to accept the things I couldn't change, as the Serenity Prayer says."

"So that's it. You've accepted defeat before you've even tried to make a go of it with us?"

She gave a resigned shake of her head.

"Benjamin, the progress you wanted so desperately is being accomplished between you and Ethan. You have everything you need to realize your dreams. I'd just be a burden you'd regret one day."

She was dismissing him again, using the tragedy of her past to wave away the role she played in their lives as if it were smoke from a snuffed out candle. Well, he and Ethan would not be waved away.

"You know what I think, Doctor Stone? I think you've settled into analysis paralysis. You've created this safe little zone for yourself where you can rescue people, come and go through their lives, depending on the day of the week, and then move on without having to stick around for the long haul. And that's not the heart of who you are. That's not the person I'd want for my rock."

Ali stood slowly as if the day's work had increased the torque on all her muscles. She turned her face away and walked toward the edge of the park, not glancing back.

Simba came to her feet, nudged her long nose against Ben's clasped hands and rested her head against his knee. He settled a palm gently behind her ears, felt the solid strength of her neck and knew if she wanted to take off a digit with her powerful jaws, she could. The animal shuddered with the force of her sigh, a sound that told him she felt his pain.

"Simba, come," Ali called.

Simba's dark eyes raked Ben's face. She tossed her head, an invitation. He leaned down and accepted the rough touch of her tongue as it gently lapped his jaw, only once, a single kiss goodbye.

Ali hadn't even done that.

He'd been afraid of the wrong female all along.

"Josie, what if he's right?" Ali asked as she poured coffee into a smiley face mug. "What if I've been telling myself I've got things under control when the truth is I've been setting limits for years on how deeply I'm willing to get involved?"

She kept remembering the boy who'd taken his life. Had she failed him with her emotional distance? Then there were her Sunday Kids. Had she conveniently pigeon-holed the amount of help she could give them, accepting their futures as outside of her influence?

"Oh, that's hogwash, boss. Look at me, will ya? If you hadn't helped me get my GED and apply for nursing school, given me that job and let me bunk with you I'd still be on the streets. If that's not getting involved I don't know what is.

"And would it be so horrible if you did discover your feet stink like everybody else's? That you're not immune to weakness after all?

Isn't this what you psychotherapists call a *breakthrough?*"

Ali smiled as she settled on the other stool at her kitchen counter and set her mug on the granite surface.

"Good point, girlfriend." Ali slipped an arm around Josie's shoulders and gave a loving squeeze. "Nobody ever explained it quite that clearly in med school."

"Hey, glad I could help." Josie gave a humble nod before continuing. "You didn't ask for my opinion, but I think you need to spend some time talking about this stuff with your little sister. Her childhood wasn't as jacked up as yours but her memories could probably use some analysis, too. Just promise me you'll pray about it, okay, boss?"

Once again Ali was taken aback by the good sense and maturity of this streetwise young woman who was working so hard to make something of her life. Maybe Erin could handle the whole truth after all. And in sharing that truth Ali would be releasing a burden she'd been carrying since she'd done the only thing she knew to protect her baby sister.

Maybe it was time for the role reversal to come full circle, to let the younger one be the stronger one.

"How did you get to be so smart, Josie?"

A wry chuckle set the stage for her honesty. "On the street it's be smart or die. You can't run from the truth, you can't keep looking back all the time and you can't depend just on yourself. You have to depend on God and sometimes a few other people who can help you see how this relationship thing gets all fouled up.

"Maybe God's done the same for you, boss. Maybe He put the football star and his kid into your life to free you from leaning on your own understanding."

Ali turned her face to the kitchen window. The sun was halfway to China, leaving the Texas sky black, bleak. She could consider Josie's words until the morning light crept across the floor again and it wouldn't change a thing. She still wasn't worthy of a Congressman's love.

Chapter Twenty-Two

Ali was a survivor. She'd outlasted the nightmare that was her childhood and then a string of anything-but-loving foster homes. She'd come through eight years of study and struggle indebted to banks and teachers, but she'd made it.

She was also a natural caregiver, still hoped to be a mother someday. Ali believed her mission in life was to help others. Her professional door was always open and her work with West Texas Rescue took priority over personal interests. She knew her strengths and used them for the good of others.

Yet, in the past twenty-four hours the Holy Spirit had led her to a new discovery: all her experience, learning, activity and busyness had been an effective method for dodging the person who most needed honest attention.

Alison Stone.

She couldn't change what had happened with Benjamin, but she would find a way to make use of the heartache she was feeling today. To turn this dreadful aloneness into something positive for the future, for what was left of her family.

Her feet were lead weights as she trudged the last fifty yards through the woods of Halfway Landing toward her destination. Her spirit was equally heavy from a sleepless night and the morning's worship service spent in prayer instead of praise.

Father, let me truly open myself to those you place in my path today. Let me use this broken-ness in my heart to relate to the needs of others. Don't let me be alone, Lord. Send someone who can love me in my strength and my weakness.

Simba whined. She strained against the leash, unhappy at being tethered.

"I know," Ali comforted. "You're excited about seeing the Sunday Kids, but we're a little early."

The tugging intensified.

"Okay, you talked me into it." Ali leaned

down and unhooked the clasp. "We're almost there anyway."

Simba shot through the underbrush, dodging trees, a missile seeking her target.

Her deep barking echoed in the silent wood and Ali smiled for the first time that day. "I guess Lenny and the girls are already here."

Moments later Ali took the final turn into the makeshift clearing. The greeting she was about to shout lodged in her throat, became a painful silence. Only a stone's throw away, an unexpected sight stole her breath and her heart.

Benjamin!

He was leaning against the fallen tree where she'd eaten her lunch a week earlier. Seated before him, Simba watched intently, studied the odd picture Benjamin made holding up the trembling hand signal for *'sit.'* He repeated it over and over as if by doing so she'd continue to obey.

"How many times do you want her to sit?" Ali called.

"Just the once. How do I tell her to stay put?"

"Stop waving your arm and hold your palm in front of her face. She'll understand."

He followed instructions.

"Now motion toward the ground one time with your palm down."

Simba rewarded him by dropping to her belly but remained alert for more signals.

As Ali got closer the progressive reddening of his face indicated he was holding his breath.

"You did great. Now breathe!"

He groaned along with the exhale as the pent-up carbon dioxide whooshed from his lungs, but he never took his gaze off Simba. "You sure she won't run at me again?"

"I'll protect you," Ali teased as she reached his side.

Benjamin slipped an arm around her waist, pulled her against his chest and buried his face in her hair as he ran his other hand down the length of her back. Her arms drifted around his strong body, rested secure as if they were created for his embrace.

"I don't think she ran at you in the first place," Ali whispered. "If anything she ran to you. She's learned to care for you."

"How about you, Ali? Could you learn to care for me?"

She squeezed her eyelids, gripped him close. Hoped to get the words past her lips? Prayed he would welcome them?

"I'm way past that point, Benjamin," she murmured. "I love you."

He brought his hands to her face, tipped her head back and held her cheeks so she would look into eyes the color of heaven.

"Say it again," his plea was desperate. "I need to hear it once more."

"I love you," she repeated. "I fell for you the night you cheated at Scrabble to help your son. I knew right then and there you were a man after my own heart."

Benjamin lowered his face, pressed his cheek to hers. "Ali, honey, I adore you more than I ever thought possible. Please, *please* give us a chance to be a family."

The words murmured against Ali's neck sent shivers down her bare arms. She tightened her embrace, her hands pulling him closer. He wound his arms around her shoulders.

"You're not repulsed by what I told you last night?"

"Of course I am, but not in the way you expected. I'm repulsed by what you endured at the hands of your father. I'm repulsed that we live in a world where that perversity is rampant. And I'm disgusted with myself for being so wrapped up in my own life that I failed to figure it all out on my own."

She wanted to look up into his rugged face, but when she tried to step back his arms tightened.

"Don't push me away, please," his voice broke. "I love your courage and your spirit. I love your grubby boots, your dangly earrings, your freckles and even your dog. But mostly I love the woman you are, the purity of your heart. Say you'll come home to Ethan and me."

He kissed the top of her head, loosened his hold, allowed her to put an inch between them.

"Benjamin, tell me the truth. Is this about the two of us or the three of us?"

"Ali, I have a son so there will always be three of us. More if you want to bring some of your other Sunday Kids into our lives. But this—" he motioned back and forth with his hand "—this will always be just about the two of us. These last weeks have shown me I don't need anything else to be complete."

"What about the Congressional race?"

He shook his head, no trace of sadness in his face. "I called Randy, told him no go."

"How'd he take it?"

Benjamin chuckled. "He blew a head gasket, called me everything but a friend of the family."

"And you think that's funny?" She couldn't help wondering at Benjamin's odd reaction.

"Ironic funny, yeah. But only because it confirmed what I'd suspected, that my *good buddy* tipped off the paper to send out that photographer. Randy thought he'd force my hand, show me how badly I wanted the public's approval. But the truth is he always wanted this more than me."

"But what about your family, their ambition for you? Is that all somebody else's idea, too?"

"No, I still want to serve, that's something I feel way down inside." He patted his mid-section. "But I've been going about this all wrong, getting the cart before the horse."

"How do you mean?"

Benjamin showed her by once again sliding his hands around her waist, lacing his fingers behind her back and rocking her gently while he gazed down, emotion gleaming in his eyes, shining from the depths of his spirit.

"Ali, my family name didn't get me into the NFL. It took years of learning my sport before I was any good at it. Just like you, I had to study and practice and give myself to it heart, mind and body before I became a professional. I need to do the same with public service, if I want to be taken seriously. It was presumptu-ous of me to expect to start at the top instead of humbling myself as a true servant should. I want to be respected for the things I do today, not the game I played in another lifetime. That's why I'm asking for your help."

Her heart thumped. She took a step back, braced herself for the role he was about to ask her to fill, fearful it was not at all what she wanted for her life.

"C'mere darlin' girl." The natural drawl he worked to keep out of his speech slid into place as he spread his hands in invitation. She leaned closer. He slipped one arm behind her back, pinned her to him, then crooked her chin in his hand.

It was warm, solid, comforting. Like Benjamin.

"You have underestimated us both. You're a woman worth pursuing and I'm a man who doesn't give up. I'm going to show up everywhere you go, so you might as well make my presence at your side official, starting right now."

"What did you have in mind?" She melted against him. *Please God, don't let me act like a desperate thirty-something female.*

"Be my teacher," he said simply. "Show me how to be patient and kind, to dig beneath the surface of problems and find true solutions, just like you do."

"Ooookay." She stiffened a bit, swallowed down her disappointment. Teacher. Hmm. What was she expecting, anyway?

"There's more." He gave her a little shake, a loosen up jiggle. "Be my partner in service. Help me see the need in our community, in the kids of this city. Partner with me to find ways to meet those needs."

"Sure." She felt her eyes begin to sting. A rush of emotions clogged her throat. He cared about the things that mattered most to her.

"Be Ethan's friend," he touched his forehead to Ali's, their eyes downcast to the spot where their hearts hammered in one rhythm. "He needs you in his life as much as he needs me, if not more."

Her pulse thudded a painful beat. Would Benjamin ever see her other than as a therapist, a caregiver?

"I'll be there for as long as you want me," she whispered, afraid he'd hear the trembling of her voice.

"And that's where I'm in trouble, baby." Benjamin crooked her chin upward. She looked into the bottomless depths of his eyes and saw her future.

"I want you forever. I want you for my wife.

I want you beside me in everything I do from this day forward. I promise that if you'll honor me with your trust, I'll earn it with my faithfulness, every day for the rest of my life."

There were no words for a fitting response. So, Ali lifted her face and offered Benjamin her kiss. All of her kisses for the rest of her life.

And in her heart she offered God thanks for her forever family.

* * * * *

Dear Reader,

I learned some sad and frightening statistics as I researched child abuse in America. An estimated 900,000 children are victims of abuse and neglect every year, with approximately four fatalities every single day.

By age twenty-one, 80% of young adults who had been abused meet the criteria for at least one psychiatric disorder such as depression or anxiety.

Children who experience abuse are 28% more likely to be arrested as adults and 30% more likely to commit violent crimes.

In the United States, 14.4% of all men and 36.7% of all women in prison were sexually abused as children. And we're not talking about teenagers in consensual relationships. The median age for sexual abuse is just nine years old.

Unbelievable statistics, aren't they? But there are tremendous efforts being made to break this cycle through (1) services that support families, (2) education on prevention for adults and children and (3) promoting the notion that stopping child abuse is *everyone's* business.

Christ said, "I tell you the truth, whatever you did for one of the least of these brothers of mine, you did for me."

Get involved. Visit Web sites such as

www.preventchildabuse.org

or contact your state office of Child Protective Services for more information. A child's safety is an adult's job.

Until we meet again, let your light shine.

Mac Nunn

QUESTIONS FOR DISCUSSION

1. Once a little-known disorder, autism now affects 1 in every 166 children in the United States. Why do you think the incidence of this disorder is on the rise?

2. Asperger's syndrome is a highly functioning form of autism. Have you ever been exposed to a child or adult with Asperger's? What was your experience?

3. Ali and her sister responded to their abusive childhood quite differently—one by running away from family and the other by studying family. Which reaction would you be most likely to have? Why?

4. Benjamin led a charmed life until tragedy struck, first in the diagnosis of his son and then in the death of his wife. Who do you believe is better equipped to deal with personal loss, women or men? Explain why you feel the way you do.

5. Ali went into the foster care system at the age of twelve. How much do you know

about foster care in your city or state? Would you consider being a foster parent?

6. Ben's post-football career was as a motivational speaker who espoused the power of positive thinking. Do you agree that a positive attitude about life can change your circumstances? Have an impact on your future?

7. I have a dear friend whose daughter wrestles daily with OCD and anxiety disorders. Much of what their family has been through inspired me to write Ethan's character. Do you know a person or family struggling with mental illness? Are you praying for them and helping them to cope in some way?

8. Ben told Ali about a time in his career as a professional football player when he felt people only cared about him for his athletic ability. Why do you think our society is so enamored of high-profile sports figures?

9. Ali was a volunteer with West Texas Rescue and she specialized in helicopter

long line operations. We've all watched those amazing videos of stranded people being plucked off the tops of cars and houses just before flood waters sweep them away. Have you ever wondered about the men and woman who risk their lives by volunteering to save strangers in life-threatening situations?

10. Ben found that blind faith in a friend was probably not such a good thing. Has there been a time in your life when you trusted a friend or family member without question and lived to regret it?

11. Ali dedicated her professional life to working with abused kids. Have you ever taken the time to research child abuse in America? Commit to spending ten minutes on the Internet and then discuss your results with your friends or reader group.

12. Ali was grateful to have a second chance for a relationship with her little sister, Erin. But even the best of sibling relationships can be trying at times. Can you relay a situation with a sister or brother that almost made you lose your religion?

13. There are some extremely difficult sibling relationships that seem impossible to overcome. But nothing is impossible with our God. Was there ever a time when you sought spiritual guidance to resolve a dispute with a brother or sister?

14. Are you new to Love Inspired books or have you been reading them for years? Are you aware we now have historical and suspense as well as contemporary novels?

Please visit www.LoveInspiredAuthors.com. We'd love to hear from you!

Here's a sneak peek at
THE WEDDING GARDEN
by Linda Goodnight,
the second book in her new miniseries
REDEMPTION RIVER,
available in May 2010 from Love Inspired.

One step into the living room and she froze again, pan aloft.

A hulking shape stood in shadow just inside the French doors leading out to the garden veranda. This was not Popbottle Jones. This was a big, bulky, dangerous-looking man. She raised the pan higher.

"What do you want?"

"Annie?" He stepped into the light.

All the blood drained from Annie's face. Her mouth went dry as saltines. "Sloan Hawkins?"

The man removed a pair of silver aviator sunglasses and hung them on the neck of his black rock-and-roll T-shirt. He'd rolled the sleeves up, baring muscular biceps. A pair of eyes too blue to define narrowed, looking her over as though he were a wolf and she a bunny rabbit.

Annie suppressed an annoying shiver.

It was Sloan, all right, though older and with more muscle. His nearly black hair was shorter now—no more bad-boy curl over the forehead—but bad boy screamed off him in waves just the same. He was devastatingly handsome, in a tough, rugged, manly kind of way. The years had been kind to Sloan Hawkins.

She really wanted to hate him, but she'd already wasted too much emotion on this outlaw. With God's help she'd learned to forgive. But she wasn't about to forget.

Will Sloan and Annie's faith be strong
enough to see them through
the pain of the past and allow them to open
their hearts to a possible future?
Find out in THE WEDDING GARDEN
by Linda Goodnight,
available May 2010 from Love Inspired.

Love Inspired® SUSPENSE

RIVETING INSPIRATIONAL ROMANCE

Watch for our new series of
edge-of-your-seat suspense novels.
These contemporary tales
of intrigue and romance
feature Christian characters
facing challenges to their faith...
and their lives!

NOW AVAILABLE IN REGULAR & LARGER-PRINT FORMATS

**Steeple
Hill®**

Visit:
www.SteepleHill.com